P etra Kuppers' *Ice Bar* often defies clean  futurism, fantasy, myth, steampunk, magical realism, and more. Kuppers' poetic prose moves viscerally quick with its rich description and surreal details that leave you balancing on the edge of reality and something, somewhere else—a dream, a hallucination, a false memory. Importantly, the worlds of Kuppers' stories are worlds with not only mermaids, ghosts and other non-human beings, but also worlds full of disabled people, queer people, and people of color whose narratives are not about their disability, sexuality, gender, or race alone. The politics of the texts are clear, yet unobtrusive, integrated into not merely content, but also the aesthetics of the collection. Take the plunge and escape into the ever-shifting worlds of *Ice Bar*.

SAMI SCHALK, AUTHOR OF *BODYMINDS REIMAGINED: (DIS)ABILITY, RACE, AND GENDER IN BLACK WOMEN'S SPECULATIVE FICTION*

E ach story in *Ice Bar* unsettles the reader as Kuppers' writing seamlessly slides between the familiarity of the present into strange apocalyptic visions and hidden dream worlds. Woven throughout the collection are the grounding touchstones of adaptation and interdependence, community, and raw human connection. *Ice Bar* elegantly expresses Kuppers' dedication to creating art that entertains while thoughtfully fostering inclusivity and social justice.

KATHRYN ALLAN, CO-EDITOR, *ACCESSING THE FUTURE: A DISABILITY-THEMED ANTHOLOGY OF SPECULATIVE FICTION*

I n Petra Kuppers' marvelously inventive collection of short stories, we journey from a post-apocalyptic world of fire and ice to a world where graveyard lichen from abandoned mental hospitals is smoked, calling back the dreams and nightmares of dead inmates. Past and present, human and animal, swim and swirl together here. Kuppers' stories are grounded in disability culture, and they send down wild roots and sprout branches which twist and curl.

ANNE FINGER, AUTHOR OF *CALL ME AHAB*

Ice Bar

Petra Kuppers

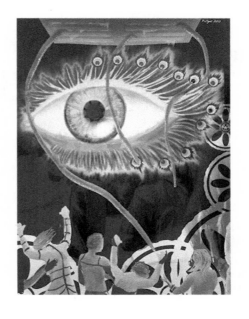

SPUYTEN DUYVIL
New York City

Acknowledgements

"Dolphin Pearls" *Dark Matter* (2017)
"The Wheelchair Ramp" *Anomaly/Drunken Boat* (2017)
"Fjord Pool" *The Dunes Review* (2017)
"Ice Bar" *PodCastle* (2017)
"Grave Weed" *Capricious* (2017)
"Dumpling's Pillar" *Mrs Rochester's Attic*. Ed. Matthew Pegg. Mantle Arts Press (2017)
"Painting in the Asylum Garden" *Sycamore Review* 28:1 (2017)
"The Road Under the Bay" *The Future Fire* (2016)
"River Crossing" *The Future Fire* (2017)
"Playa Song" *Accessing the Future: A Disability-Themed Anthology of Speculative Fiction*.
Eds. Djibril al-Ayad and Kathryn Allan (2015)
"Pool Shark" *Flash Fiction* (2017)
"The Nursing Home" *Wordgathering* (2014)
"Dinosaur Dreams" Deaf Poets Society, "Crips in Space" special issue (2017), reprinted in
inaugural issue of Opaline Magazine, "Resist!" special issue (2017)

© Petra Kuppers
ISBN 978-1-944682-93-4
Cover art by Miranda Jean, "A giant blue eye. Water color. Peacock feather
eyelashes. Party people, of all color, of all shapes. Torture/pleasure/pain.
BDSM scene. Gears or wheelchair wheels. Tentacles. Prostheses. Embrace
and support. Organic mechanics, an air conditioner, hints of infrastructure.
Human animal plant hybrids."

Library of Congress Cataloging-in-Publication Data

Names: Kuppers, Petra, author.
Title: Ice bar / Petra Kuppers.
Description: New York City : Spuyten Duyvil, [2018]
Identifiers: LCCN 2017038935 | ISBN 9781944682934
Classification: LCC PS3611.U6458 A6 2018 | DDC 813/.6--dc23
LC record available at https://lccn.loc.gov/2017038935

CONTENTS

I. STEAM

ICE BAR

She emerged into the bright sunshine, some daynight after. She looked up to the sky, some daynight after. The sun looked different somehow, not doubled exactly, but there was a too-muchness in the air. And a new color to the shadows on the ground. The shadows were smaller, unfamiliar.

Alissa took off her jacket, her sweater, all the things she had grabbed fleeing. In bra and underwear she stalked like a crane through the window opening and into the Oslo street. The sun began to burn immediately. She felt the sizzle of her skin's moisture, like a hot-plate drop of wax. Quickly, she ducked into the shadows on the other side of the street. A hairdresser had abandoned their studio. The smashed windows were not boarded up again, and shards of glass lay mingled with strands of long straight black hair on the linoleum. Alissa saw the hair, stopped. She flashed back to Jin's slender form, the willow waistline that had held her fascination for weeks before she approached her fellow student. Jin had smiled, giggled a bit, when Alissa had asked her for a drink, for a date. That had been seven months ago. Where would Jin be now? A city away, a continent, across a fjord or in the heavens?

Alissa picked up her drooping shoulders and willed her feet to move further back into the darkly shadowed hair studio. There was nothing fruitful in reminiscing about scents and sweet touches here, in the half-light of a new too-bright day. In recent daynight periods she had found herself often staying too long, steps and gazes halted by small moments, tiny monuments to the life before. Stop moving and stare, a good way to get kicked in the butt by sunlight or radiation.

In the back of the studio Alissa found another survivor. A woman in a sheepskin's wrap had made a nest for herself beneath the skeletons of the retro hair-dryers, hulking shapes of pink and red plastic, upside-down bowls to encompass freshly washed and laid waves. It was hard to imagine the hair dryers in use, but they fit right in: flamingos staking out territory, hipster citations for new androgynies.

The woman uncurled a little bit when Alissa cleared her throat and said a dry, raspy hello.

"Hello. Please move along. There is nothing here. The water is shut off."

"Okay. I am not here to hurt you, lady. And I have my own water. What do you plan to do here?"

"I am at home. I am fine. Please move along."

One of the hopeless ones. Alissa had met them underground, little broken ones that did not wish to live past the apocalypse, who saw the demise of internet, telephony and petrol-driven life as a reason to hasten their own demise, too. A valid choice, of course. Alissa nodded, and started to move along.

"Oh, one thing. Did others come by?"

"Two, the day before. One, the day it happened. You are the first one since."

"Thanks. Die well, lady."

Alissa moved past the felt nest and found the backdoor of the hair studio. She opened it carefully, peered out. She had been alert to any news, but hadn't heard about vigilantes, the much-talked-about breakdown of human compassion and morals. Actually, people had been kinder to each other recently, had shared water, even scraps of food. The tunnels had been terrible, but not because of the people. It was the smell that got her out eventually, the hot smell and the press of it all. Also, curiosity. What did it look like above, now that the sun had shifted and found companions? It had been a choice: heat death or cave death. No one had imagined other options or real viable life after. That meant, probably, that she wasn't that different from nest lady. Alissa stepped out of the backdoor, shouting 'Hi' to whomever could hear her.

A 'Hi' came back. Her ears pricked. But it came back more than once. Just an echo, vibrations reverberating human-like against the steel plates of the modernist apartment buildings. The courtyard in Oslo's Toyen district was shiny and hot like an oven. No one was hanging out here now. Alissa moved on, through the arc at the far end of the yard, and into the next street.

Cars, tires melted and glued to the asphalt. Small curls of smoke where car mirrors set spots to smoldering. No other movement in the blue air. Above, blinding light: the sun or, maybe, suns had climbed higher, whiteness taking over any shape or contour. Alissa sprinted across the street, ran along the opposite side, where some shade remained. Ran because stopping would mean unsticking her sneakers from the molten pavement. So she touched lightly, taking note of the stores she passed, looking for something to arrest the inevitable. In a gap between buildings, she looked down at the city center and the fjord, its bare dry walls bone white, salt flowers over gravel. What had been green looked burned, black mud, or grey like ash. She turned away, laid her hands against the warm yellow bricks of new houses.

The sign shone above her, sparkled in the sunlight. Ice bar. Ice bar? Alissa stopped, pressed quickly against the black door, and felt it give. It was open. Down she went.

As soon as she entered, she could feel the coolness waft up from beneath. A café scene behind blackout windows. Blond people nearby, short hair, layered at the back, a careful cut above jeans jackets, printed T-shirts. Tight jeans. 20-some-things. An older woman, close-cropped hair white-blond with dark roots. An expensive parka, leather bag, Doc Martens. Next to her, a young man, brown long wavy hair over John Lennon glasses, a mustache that dripped across the cheekbones. Long coat. A pagan cross. He turned to her.

"Welcome. Do you need water?"

He held out a slender glass bottle, real glass with a wavy design, condensation shimmering the surface. She accepted and nearly fainted with the crispness of contact. It was so cool! She hadn't felt anything like it for weeks. She touched the round glass opening to her lips and reveled in the deliciousness of liquid down her throat. Careful now. She mustn't get carried away. She stopped. Sighed.

"First time here, right? Welcome to the Ice Bar."

"Thank you. Thank you." Alissa was near tears. He knew. She collected herself.

"What is going on here?" This was one of the old Oslo winter haunts: the site of a bar made of ice, mid-winter, usually closed in other seasons. But here she was, and yes, there were icicles dripping down from the dark ceiling. She saw her breath in front of her face. She was crying now, and the tears became salt on her skin.

"Ice Bar. Dance on the volcano. We will survive. Dance the freaking music baby."

His pupils were wide and dark pools. She got it.

She released her gaze from his, and scanned the crowd, still holding on to the magic of the cool glass bottle. Alissa remembered the bar from different years. In the deep Norwegian winter, the bar was usually made out of iceblocks, an igloo in the city shimmering blue-green with lights set into the blocks. Hipster bar. Also, a tourist pleaser. An easy pick-up spot. All that. She couldn't remember ever seeing the bar open outside winter time, and in artificial refrigeration. But here it was, pulsing with light and heaving bodies. She pushed to the front of the crowd. Everybody was grooving along, "Karma Chameleon" blasting full-force from the front, vibrating her ears the closer she got to the stage. And there was Boy George, Norwegian-style.

He was round, dark blond hair like whips drenched in sweat, waves of delicious flesh touched with a hint of blue frost. Crotchless pleather pants opened to a large black rubber dildo beating along to the music. Two lines of criss-cross laces ran up over bulging flesh to a military bra cupping abundance. A small pencil mustache over red lips. He crooned and swayed with the song, Karaoke'd with a swish, fastfastfastslow. This close up by the stage, Alissa was surrounded by adoration, the drag king's entourage in happy 80's flow. Silver lamé flashed in blond and black hair, blue eyeshadows draped across freckled rosy noses and, here and there, chocolate skin. Goosebumps embroidered shaking limbs. She took another draft of her cold water bottle and tried to make eye contact. No go: all pupils wide and lost in the charm of the music. She pushed to the left of the stage, to the curtained-off area between the well-stocked bar and the runway.

The music followed her but the light and cold did not. It was more mellow here in the shadows. Up ahead, Alissa saw the next performer getting ready. She approached, ready to try again to ascertain the meaning of this ritual and its connection to the sun death outside.

"Hello."

"Hello." The answering voice was mellow, with a hint of kindness, interested. It emerged from a wrapped form lying on what looked like an autopsy table: stainless steel without grab bars, a wheeled contraption on high shine. The small woman had just transferred to the table and her wheelchair was standing idle alongside, like a pony having a rest. She was arranging a sheepskin beneath herself, tucking small limbs onto the fleecy surface and away from the steel bite.

"I just got in here. Why is this place refrigerated? What is going on?"

"Can you tuck this piece over there? My partner seems to have lost their way from the bathroom."

Alissa complied, gently folding a piece of suede under a creamy tiny thigh. The flesh was warm, pliant, and she felt a thrill run through her. The performer noticed.

"Come with me, newbie. Come onto the stage and sing. You'll see and find your answers."

She extended a small, perfectly formed arm, dimples at the elbow. Her fingernails were painted dark green with sparkles. Alissa took her hand.

Boy George came off the stage in a rush of sound and applause, screams echoing into the curtained corridor. He dahling'ed his way past them, into the far bowels of the bar, into the dark. Alissa could see blood dripping down his bare back from scratches that had opened the corset laces. The small woman next to her tugged at her hand.

"I am Minerva. It's our turn. Just follow."

And Minerva directed her to push the autopsy table down the corridor. A helper appeared suddenly from the depth, a hummingbird creature in lilac and purple eye-shadow over soft brown eyes and skin. Batting eyelashes, they directed Alissa to push and laid their own long pale blue fingernails alongside Alissa's splintered messes. Together they trundled the autopsy table up the wheelchair ramp to the stage. That's as far as the hummingbird went. Releasing the table, they walked backward after depositing their tiara on Alissa's head.

Minerva directed Alissa to position her in the network of stage lights. She bathed in the beams. Her little limbs moved fluidly through the air, pointing to where she wanted Alissa to push. Finally she was bidden to drop the brakes on the wheels. When Alissa straightened from her task, a new person had arrived on stage, a flash of sequined tubes, with a microphone in their hands. Alissa took the proffered mic, and Minerva invited her to hold it close to her small rosebud lips. Minerva breathed into the mic, and for the first time, Alissa became aware of the audience beyond their bright stage. The breath had pulled them in, forward, with the out-breath from the little mouth releasing a wave of relaxation across the wide Ice Bar. It rippled out all the way to the guy with the long hair who had given Alissa her water. She could see him, quiet and dark, a greeter on the threshold. He seemed to nod at her. She refocused, and, listening to an in-breath from Minerva, saw the crowd lean in toward them, eagerly waiting.

Music. Flashing lights. Minerva opened her lips, and "Smooth Operator" ballooned into flight. Alissa just held the mic, still and solid. From time to time, Minerva laid her tiny hand on Alissa's arm, emphasizing a sighing moment in the song's unspooling. The crowd was blissful. Swaying creatures lined the edges of the stage walkway beyond the sharp edges of the autopsy table.

The song ended. Minerva closed her perfect eyes, eye shadow in peacock stripes sending light signals into the universe. The crowd went wild. Applause and shouts. Alissa saw them, and saw beyond, too: the giant air conditioner chugging and heaving high in the vaulted ceiling. It shuddered and waved electric lines out toward the crowd and the singer. Minerva sucked in air through her perfect pout, and Alissa watched one of the cables lash forward, toward them, and sink electric wires like fangs into a fan's back. A small man, white skin under leather doublet, heavy boots. She jumped back with a tiny hop, but Minerva had fastened a small hand on hers and steadied her. The crowd kept shouting, undulating, and Alissa could see the caught fan wriggling in ecstasy on the live wire, not two meters from the stage. Then the wire released with drips of red blood, and coiled back to the ceiling.

The crowd shifted down a notch, calmed themselves. Some turned to their drinks. The dripee staggered a bit, Alissa saw, but kept upright, facial grimace unreadable: pain or pleasure? He looked a tad pale, stunned but ok. When he turned Alissa could see the jagged scratches where the cable had taken its bite. The doublet had shredded decoratively along the back, weaving a new pattern of skin and leather strips. Ignoring his bleeding back, the man took a beer someone had offered, glass

9

dewy with cool condensation, and drank deeply.

Minerva signaled to Alissa to undock the autopsy table's wheels. She took a small bow, blew a kiss into the crowd. Then the hummingbird was back, and the two of them guided Minerva's chariot down the ramp.

That daynight, after the lights went out, Alissa shivered on the floor. Hummingbird had given her a blanket, something that looked like it might have been one of Minerva's sitting blankets. Lambswool, small tight curls, pressed and shaped into hollows and rises, near bald in spots, but still fine to cover herself with as she curled into sleep. She listened to the wind in her lungs, the in and out of her own cave breath, and touched the knot of fear deep inside.

er

Alissa stayed at the Ice Bar. She became an act with Minerva and Hummingbird, and refined her costume. Instead of her black bra and panties over sneakers, she added combat boots, and found a different bra, with a netted back, on a recently passed woman in one of the dungeons beneath the Bar. Every night the air conditioner drank its fill of patrons and performers alike. It seemed fair to Alissa, in the harsh lights of blue and pink ice days: everything needs fuel, and humans had used up their allocation. Why not be fuel, and enjoy the process of heating one's self to the right temperature? Dancing away, they were little cool ice cream bonbons with molten warm hearts, disco balls of liquid delight.

The performances died down a few hours after the heat of the day, and punters and team alike just went to sleep where they stood, curling limbs into one another for dream safety. After that, in what would have been late afternoon or early evening in the prior-time, a crew came round with sandwiches. No questions were answered, and so she stopped asking: what meat is this? Where did the bread come from? Why does this taste so salty? It came, and then the performances started up again. All the while, they stayed cool, and no one, no one at all, re-emerged from the front door, and saw the street again. In the few hours of dusk/dawn openness, a bit of wanderlust might lead one to the toilets, to the warren of tunnels beneath the stage, to the dark round holes that seemed to lead to other houses. But no one went to check on the street and the open air beyond. That life was gone, and done, behind a crystal rainbow curtain.

σ

Tonight was the night. Her first solo act. Alissa was nervous, and tight with pulse and feelings. Minerva had been the one who told her.

"The management thinks you are ready. I think so, too. Go out and wow them, babe. Do you want to use my make-up chest?"

Everybody was so friendly, so sharing. Alissa couldn't even remember ever having seen so many lipsticks, eye shadows, liners and false lashes in one place. She opened box after box, trying to decide on her new look. She had already found a piece of music in the karaoke box: "Private Dancer." That was the one. So now she wanted to do a Thunderdome look to go with that, blackwhite whiteblack outback queen. She assumed this to be a command performance, a one and only. She was ready for her swan song, to lift into the cool moon.

The nightday. The stage. Minerva and Hummingbird kissed her. Boy George gave her a wax flower, a dark purple day lily which shaded into black. She clipped it into her short curly hair. They all touched her, braille love on her bare skin, new-old family. She smiled and released the last smell of fear from deep in her lung wings. She let her fear fly, ascend in her thorax, up through the windpipe, and when she finally stepped into the light, the crowd, the song, her mouth broke open and it flew and flew and touched the snake's sweet mouth and then they were one, the bird and the snake and the lung and the cave and the planet and the sun, under the Thunderdome.

Later that nightday, after her flight, Alissa rested in Hummingbird's brown sinewy arms. A tattoo of a kiwi bird was by her nose, a kiwi that had stepped out from an impossibly dense bush, and had lifted its long nosebeak toward the moon. Alissa felt the pulse in the back, the crusty densing of knitting flesh and blood. She felt an island of peace seep from the open delta, new parts of land rise from salt and sea in the solar plexus, a liver sifting and shielding, kidneys to winnow old and new. Minerva had come by for a while, in her small pink wheelchair, and had brought warm tea, a delicacy here in the land of cold. Alissa had felt the surge of blood tide in the salty warmth. They would go on, soaking and receding, filtering into the electric purity of the snake's mouth. They would worship the cool moon. Outside, the neon sign was still lit, in the never-darkness of daynight, flickering into the stillness of the dust street. Here was the Ice Bar, harbor, ocean.

GRAVE WEED

She found the book in the small bookstore of the rejuvenated Traverse City State Hospital grounds. In the window, the store had beckoned to her with *Stories of the Mental Hospital*, old sepia-colored photos on a spread with tiny, barely legible print. An amateur production crammed full of historical details garnered with obsession and love. She stared at the open book in the window, and imagined herself holding it. The pages, glossy and quite stiff, turning them slowly, reading with the loupe she had inherited from her grandma. Marcia entered.

Inside, the storekeeper saw her but stayed behind his small counter. He wasn't pushy. She turned this way and that, fondled bindings, even lifted some older books to her nose to smell their breath. There were only two aisles in the small store, and she had come to the end of the first one when it happened. A hairy brown hand crawled through the gap between two sections (Local History and Lake Seafaring). Marcia jumped a tiny bit inside before realizing that this was another customer, groping for something in the empty air. She turned the corner, and saw the man in the next aisle. Hairy, like his hand. A bear of a man, with soft curly fur escaping from the top buttons of his green and red striped shirt. He hadn't seen her and still pawed the air behind the books on his aisle. She stood on tiptoes to see what section the bear was looking through. Another in-between. True Crime and Ghost Stories. Intriguing. Marcia stepped closer to the bear, and turned the other way, to the books on the opposite side. She knew the ways of booksellers, knew how they stacked the stacks when all was full or overflowing. Maybe there was something here, tucked into the open shelf that followed on from aborted Maternal Self-Help. Indeed, some books lounged there which didn't seem part of this label. One could be, she guessed, if the bookseller had a weird sense of humor: *Asylum Reared: The True Story of Baby Barbara*. Huh. She pulled out the book and saw that it was the memoir of a woman who lived her first years in Traverse City State Hospital, child of an unwed mother, as likely a reason as many to end up in the thick walls of the institution. She put the book back.

Her hand brushed against its neighbor, its spine broken and unreadable. She pulled it toward her, angled the dark cover to the light. It was more a pamphlet than a book, a little arty publication. On its cover was a grotesque sight: a grave marker, small, concrete, just a number in a field of grass. Marcia knew what this was, the conventionalized ways that asylum inhabitants were laid to rest in surrounding fields. Anonymous, easily lost, stumbling blocks for later hikers. The grave marker on the pamphlet was covered in shrill-colored lichen, pinks and greens and whites pulsating against one another. The title of the publication made her shudder. *Bones and Pearls: The Botany of Graves.*

The bear behind her must have felt the vibration creeping through her body, for he turned now, saw the pamphlet in her hand. He looked up, a stricken cast in his eye.

"Is this what you are looking for?" Marcia reached the book across, innocently.

"Yes! I've been looking for this everywhere. Thank you. I thought you were going to get it yourself."

"No worries, I am just browsing. It's freaky, though, isn't it?"

"I guess so. *Botany of Graves*. But it's also really useful. It was written by someone in my family."

"Really?" Marcia entered fluidly into the conversation, her eyes wide, knowing her pull and power. She listened as bear man explained an uncle's obsession, his journeys across the Midwest, sampling graves in old and new graveyards, his experiments in old closed-down asylums like Eloise and Traverse City.

"The theory was that some mixture of madness, medication

and exposure created mineral-rich bones, a special fertilizer for these lichen."

He had Marcia's full attention. Yes. Score.

er

Two days later, she and Bear (real name Hector Moulia) were grave-hunting, like the old days. Camera, scraper, chemicals, plastic baggies, and, for afterward, a weed pipe, were safely stored in her backpack. They wore sturdy shoes over thick socks, trouser legs stuffed into socks to give no purchase to ticks and the irritating little seedheads that held on tight. It was evening time in September, plants pumped full with the thickness of golden late-summer sun. Not as good as spring burst, maybe, but still an excellent harvesting time. They left the car not far from a Dairy Queen, on the edge of its car park, to blend in better with local crowds. From there, they hiked over the field, following the notes in the old history book, looking for the dwindling and hidden grave markers of Eloise's unfortunates. The ones that didn't get away. Not that many did. The ones that lay here, forgotten and unnamed, apart from some mileage in local art shows and among history enthusiasts who dared to pierce the madness stigma.

Marcia and Bear got lucky quickly. A straggly row of concrete nobs appeared in the weeds, and yes, there were lichen on some of them. Not Technicolor, quite, but lovely in their own right, blooming across the grey grainy surfaces in their botanical lace. When they righted themselves after scraping, they heard a familiar sound: a few rows away someone else seemed engaged in the same activity. A shadow, thin and long, a young man, it seemed, held something on a straight razor up to the dying light. Bear and Marcia averted their eyes. All kinds of folks were looking for a high, and it would not do to become too familiar. Their own meeting had been fortuitous, allowing them to find a companion without the direct involvement of botanical hallucinogens. You never know what someone will see in you.

An hour later, and a few phials and plastic baggies filled, they sat in the car park of a diner a few blocks away from their original spot at the Dairy Queen. This was going to be their first time together, their maiden journey of weed whacking. They had read Bear-ancestor's slim booklet a few times, and Bear had filled in lacking details. He had lost the book in a house fire a few years back, but remembered his whacked-out uncle and his strange experiments.

Bear worked methodically, quite fast for such a big man. He cut the scraped lichen with a razor blade, hatch, cross-hatch, sifting and winnowing. Any lumps were carefully crushed: if they were lichen, they stayed, foreign matter ejected. Cut cut cut sift sift sift. Now the matter was powder, greenish in the sodium light of the diner's evening illumination. Probably greenish in daylight, too: the medium color of the pale crust on the concrete markers. Marcia swallowed spittle, a lump of apprehension behind her chestbone. Bear mixed the powder with an acid from a small glass bottle, carefully drenching, shaking, scraping, turning the paste. It began to bubble. Quick quick onto a metal foil square, lighter, roasting the liquid away. The crust that remained was lighter in color, nearly pure white. Bear turned.

"Finished. Have a go with me?"

"Should we both go at the same time? What if it hurts us?"

"Some lichen? It'll be fine." Bear laughed, but with a note behind his bark that made Marcia look up. It might be better to go along. He was beginning to get a hint that she wasn't quite your average meth head/dope fiend/inhaler.

"Ok." He scraped the light-colored fresh powder into the opening of a small glass pipe. A pretty thing, Murano glass, dots of primary colors smeared around the translucent stem. It was only lightly used. Marcia could see a little bit of dope tar in the inner working. Bear, a good boy. Why was he doing this?

Finished. He looked at her, wordless. She took the pipe and the lighter from his hands, put the pipe to her mouth, the flame to the top hole, and inhaled.

&

A plain in the dusk. Wide open, empty tideland, mud and water till the horizon. There, a thin strip of ocean. She could hear the distant roar of the sea, and the shallow slushing of water here in the tidal flats. Salt ions in her nose, prickling in her ears, the exhilaration of wind. Marcia's naked feet stepped into the mud, squelching sand geysers between her toes. She heard them coming up behind her, up the gentle rise in her back. Thud, thud, thud. Two runners crested the dune hill, slapped their feet into the mud. Saw her. Slowed a tiny bit, a hesitation as a question mark.

Marcia looked at the two runners, skeletons in the evening light. They ran shirtless, and she wasn't sure if they were men or women. Folds of skin draped over bone, as if all flesh had abandoned them. Hairless, too. Heads like bowling balls, round and unmarked, with four holes in the front, one each at the side. Eyes, nose, mouth and ears hollow openings into stretched hide over bone. She knew she would see them again, but didn't know what to do. So she stood, nodded to them, a casual greeting on a sea plain, as if it were ok. They nodded back, picked up their speed again, and continued their sprint over the land.

They had been the advance troops. Marcia knew that. It would be better to have a game plan. She thought about it and walked back up the gentle rise, landward, found a dry spot to rest and wait. It didn't take long.

He came out of the gathering dusk, melted lilac and blue into the dunescape. A tall, thin man, fully dressed, but also hairless, features in flux. She didn't look yet, gave him a chance to assemble. He set up station next to her. A box appeared from beneath his jacket. He unscrewed something, and wooden legs spidered out. More screws, some folding, and he had an easel up, a small watercolor paper clipped to the flat surface. A field palette followed, and he dipped his brush in a small water tin, mixed pigments, and stroked bars of light onto the paper. She watched, mesmerized. And every time her head canted toward him, he had taken on more shape. The round head ball had become featured, a strong chin, tall forehead. The skin was pigmented now, a rich chocolate with darker streaks at the temple. The next time she looked, hair had emerged, curly and resilient pepper-and-salt springs. The nose had grown, too, and beautiful sensuous lips that moved as he laid down color. She looked back at the paper, and the dunes had taken shape there: heather and small twisted trees created by little runs of black water. A seagull, a white streak, angled into the wind.

"You look good, little one. I hadn't expected you to be back." His voice was as dark as she had remembered it, rolling in his chest like big bells. "What are you doing back here?"

"I want to find them, Lucius. Can't you help me again?"

He looked down at her, eyes kind but angled up now, measuring. "I don't know, now. It's good to let them rest. There are new people."

He nodded to the east, and she could make out new land features. Yes, she knew where she was. Duin en Boosch in the Netherlands, the grounds of a large psychiatric institution, in the beach space, the edges of land and sea. She had researched this place, had looked at the treatments, the staff, the philosophy of healing. And there *were* new people there, populating her vision: where the dunes shifted into scrub of limit forest, she could see hazy shapes, inmates walking slowly.

He was whispering now. "They are long gone, Cherie. Into the line. Over the edge. Let them go."

She bowed over his painting, saw the horizon line on the paper, small filigree patterns of color eating into the white paper as water found its way past dykes and polders. She leaned closer. The line opened. She fell in, his laughter at her back.

ℰ

The line is violet, feathering into red and pink at its outer edges. She is deep in the violet soup, waist deep, sinking. Round objects bob around her, and she reaches to them, tries to hold on. Her hands find one, slimy. It turns. A bowling ball skull. Teeth open wide, wide, her hand slides in, murky and shadowed, and the water turns the skull and the teeth fall.

ℰ

She shrugged up. The pipe was no longer in her hand and her head rested against the passenger window, damp cold against her pressed cheek. Bear was still out. She could see a sliver of white beneath his closed eyelids, the pipe drooping from his right hand, the lichen remnants now black as the night outside their car.

"How was it?" They drank some black coffee from the diner. Bear had struggled to wake, but had come to with a choking sound, tears leaking from his eyes. Marcia had averted her eyes, granted him privacy to get himself together. Now, coffee fumes between them, he was ready to chat. What could she say?

"Intense. Just colors, and spaces, and drifting." A very noncommittal answer, good for any drug experience, really. Bear didn't look happy. The truth creaked between them, the hunger, the need for connection. Marcia hovered on the threshold of telling him what she was searching for. But no. Too private, too painful, too weird. And she had no sense of Bear's agenda yet, either. So they let it go, over coffee, just junk-heads cruising. Till next time.

et

The next time. They were a team now, hooking up every three days or so, driving out to old institutions all over Michigan, scraping and grinding grave lichen into smoke. What they were doing was bizarre, probably dangerous, likely toxic. They knew it, and they each cursed their knotted tongues, tried so hard to speak, but by now their rhythms had settled into unspoken action. It was even harder to break open.

They were in a small graveyard, near Canton, in the Detroit suburbs. The psych unit here had been small, more a private sanatorium than a large state-run institution. But they still had their own graveyard, lists of dead inmates carefully delineated in a crumbly ledger book Marcia had found in a local going-out-of-business pawn-broker's shop. It had been one lucky find: she had traced the safe of the sanatorium to the broker, and it had stood unopened for decades. In the auction of the final sale, she had acquired the safe, about the size of an ancient transistor radio, but heavy. Bear had shown new talents as a safe-cracker by listening to the old-fashioned tumblers fall in the cylinder till the door swung open. The ledger book and a map had been on the top-most shelf, above ancient jewelry and long-silent men's watches, the spoils of the sanatorium.

So here they were, fingering crusty plant lace on top of metal markers.

They were not alone. In each abandoned graveyard they had found other searchers. Marcia remembered the young man with the straight razor, from their first joint search with Bear. He had appeared a few times more. Bear had never reacted to him, and she wasn't quite sure if that was a threshold, too, a private moment, or if that young guy was real. This time, though, Bear acknowledged his presence.

"Oi. How did you find this place?"

He sounded indignant, given all they had gone through to

find this site. The slim young man turned slightly toward them, straightened up from stooping over his own set of markers. For the first time, they could see his face. It was pale and haggard. The side Marcia hadn't seen before looked sunken even deeper, half-vanished, eaten, as if the bones in his cheek had crumpled like waxed paper, leaving little cuts on the inside of this skin. Bear took a small step back, pulled his shoulders up a little. He nodded to the guy, who kept his silence.

"Never mind," Bear grumbled half to himself, not looking up again, instead going down to scrape a fat blob of orange lichen into an envelope. "Live and let live, right, girl?"

"Right."

er

That night they met at his place. Marcia had become accustomed to him now: Bear, Hector, who lived like a poor student and wrote like a fiend. She had never tried to read in the heap of papers that threatened to fall off his desk in his studio, ignoring that mess just as she was ignoring the McDonald's bags and boxes on the kitchen counter. There were no photos anywhere, no hints of family. She sat on his bed, waiting for him to finish the preparation. She had no questions, he didn't have any demands, and that is why it worked. They just smoked, slept, and hunted for more.

Tonight the powder stayed orange for a long time. The blob from the Canton psych unit grave had an aroma all its own: a minty thing, a blast of freshness that cut through the old burger and onion haze of the studio apartment. She really liked the color, and the smell seemed familiar, unplaceable, but relaxing. She laughed a bit, opened her teeth, and Bear raised an eyebrow. Then they started. A flame. A whoosh. Inhale. First her, then Bear. But the dream wouldn't come. Instead, Marcia's mouth opened, and words flowed out.

"Mamma. Daddy. I love you. Don't leave me. Mamma. Daddy. Mamma. Come back. No. No. No. Mamma. Come back."

Marcia was astonished at the sounds that emerged from her, full of pain and sadness. She recognized herself crying, heard the voice as if she was seven years old, outside the doors of the institution, reaching thin arms through the barred gate. She blinked, embarrassed, tried to shut up, lifted her hands to shut her mouth. Closing her eyes meant that what she didn't want to see again played out on her inner eyelids. Her mother, arms reaching back, mouth askew, calling for her little girl. Her mother, dragged backward by orderlies. Her mother, who danced with butterflies and cried with crocodiles. Her mother, gone gone gone gone gone.

Marcia tried to cram her words back into her mouth, to keep from spilling the secrets to Bear, her mother's incarceration, her dad's earlier withdrawal, the time when he, too, was locked up in a white monstrosity, a different one. A glimpse over to Bear—she needn't bother with any embarrassment. No one would hold her hostage with intensity, would demand her heart from her.

For Bear was stock still himself, wide-eyed, not really seeing her, not hearing her baby talk, that sadness of longing in her voice. His mouth opened, and spilled over, staccato tones falling into the evening.

"I can look after her. Give her back to me. It will be ok. I just needed a break. Please, release her. She is my fiancé. Yes. Yes. I can take her. No, I do not have her mother's number. Yes. Yes. I can take her. Please give her to me. Please. Please. Please. Please."

Marcia saw tears dripping down Bear's face, loneliness deep in the folds that ran down from his nose to his open mouth, to the words that spilled out, the magic words that did not do their magic. He had been left alone, in a different way, by the barred gate, by the concrete marker, by the pills and the electric surge. Now she started crying too, cried for the first time in Bear's presence. This he noticed. His gaze was clear again, as if he could see her and the people he was talking to. Their mouths kept speaking, each separate, then unison, then choral.

"Mamma."

"Please."

"Mamma."

"I can take her."

"Please."

Their words mingled, overlapped, and none could stop the spillage.

et

Marcia and Bear sat in his car. Two heads, looking forward, their mouths pinned shut again, eyes pinched at the outer edges. They hadn't really decided to go back to the Canton graveyard, but both grabbed their coats as their mouths just wouldn't shut, walked to the car as if in accord, sat, and Bear turned the ignition, peeling out in that general direction, then slowing immediately to a crawl. Abeyance. Time to talk.

Bear spoke, realizing that the barrier was his to take down, his car, his apartment, his space warm and curly opening into vessel. He told Marcia about Laura, about their meeting, their love, then the withdrawals, the turns, more and more frequent, her need for solitude, his need for her safety, and the joint decision by Laura, Hector and even Laura's parents to release her into the white walls and locked corridors, just for a while, just as a raft in the drifting world, a respite for Hector, a retreat for Laura. Locks, suicide checks every fifteen minutes, the clockwork of survival space. The story bottomed out, but it had only been a plateau in Bear's confession. Down it went.

Laura had turned even further, gone quiet, so quiet, and then the bars had come down for Hector. She hadn't signed visitation forms for him, no need for that at the time, for her short visit. But then it had looped into months. The family sent him a letter. They had decided what was best. Which didn't include Hector. That was thirteen years ago. And that was all he knew. Bear ended, voice gruff, defiant.

Traffic lights reflected on the wet windows of the car. Go. Do not go. They crawled along, toward the graveyard. Marcia didn't say much.

"Yeah." She didn't know how to respond, how to make him feel better. "Yeah. That sucks." Maybe that was all that was needed. Bear seemed to hear it, and seemed ok. No tears hanging in the beard. But he wasn't ready to let it go.

"So give, girl. What is taking you on the search road? Why are you huffing grave weed?"

Marcia shrugged. It had been a long time since she put a line through it all, laid it out like pearls on a necklace, this follows that, like a reporter from the front lines. She remembered the plaintive sound of her own voice, mixed with Bear's howl, and she did not want any of it.

Bear pushed. Wheedled, even. But he was her avenue to the weed, at least for now, with car and knowledge, and he knew it. And he had spilled his, and had heard at least the sound of her voice when crying, even if he hadn't taken in the words. He didn't own her, but maybe she did owe him. Marcia weighed the ups and downs, and what it would cost her to tell her story.

Same story, really. She told it quickly, quietly, made him catch her voice from the bottom of the car's footwell.

Short rest-stops, eventually turning into a new home apart from her, first for her mother then her dad. The seduction of seclusion, of dropping everything: that's how Marcia had made sense of it for herself, knowing that at least her father had gone willingly, on his own accord. She wasn't so sure about her mum. Her mum had come back a number of times, sometimes stronger, sometimes weaker. She had dropped bits of her memory at the hospital, weeks zapped out of her brain, but she had smiled kindly again at her little girl and that was all that really mattered. But then a month on, or three, she would vanish again, drop from their lives, as if the only way to go was out. Eventually, she was gone behind the bars for good. No visits for kids in the ward.

"How long ago?" Bear stayed factual, had not leaned over or touched her. Which earned him points.

"I haven't seen my mother for twenty-two years. I do not even know if she is alive. I fell out with my other folks."

"And your dad?"

"Fifteen. He faded out, too, left the world. I could find out more about him, I think, but it was all an aftershock from her. He's gone. Some come back. Mother had made friends in the hospital, and I still see some of them around when I go and visit the neighborhood." Marcia kept her other confidantes out of it, the ones she only met on the other side of the drug veil, Lucius, others, called up by smack, or, now, much purer and clearer, in the lichen.

"And some do not. I know."

They drove on, picking up speed, the car shooting through the sparse raindrops. They arrived, parked, started to climb out. Bear reached over to Marcia, stalled her without touching her. He pulled the pipe from beneath his parka. He had more white power shimmering into green, with orange grains here and there. Yes, she nodded.

They stood in the rain, inhaling, a tang like ruby oranges on their tongues. Then they walked into the old graveyard.

er

They were not alone. Marcia swam through dune sand, ocean's edge mingling with red clay soils. Grass bent over, looped into the earth, dove away from the concrete markers and their numbers. The round hummocks rustled, stretched upward. Calvarias, skull tops, grew white and grey in the earth. A jaw emerged beneath, stretching open. A leftover dandelion trembled like a tongue in the aperture then melted into seaweed. Other skulls popped around her, round white mushrooms ready to release their spores. Marcia looked up at the other figures in the abandoned field.

Row upon row of people stood, looking down, or scanning the horizon. Silhouettes in the evening light. Some raised their arms to the moon, as if drifting. Marcia looked for faces, but all had melted. Clay in the rain. Statues made out of wet sand. Crumbling noses, yawing eye-sockets. She looked away as a woman's dress shifted back into flax fibers, weeds in the wind.

She could still make out Bear, a row over. His parka had wings now in the wind that was coming up, stretching his silhouette, opening him up. His form expanded, engulfed some of the other mourners, seekers, and Marcia wasn't sure anymore where he began and ended. She whispered to him, telling him a last secret about her mother, the secret of love, just a touch of fingers through bars. She doubted he could hear now.

She felt Lucius' hand on her neck.

"Hello little one. You are back." His voice rolled with the wind, vibrating behind her collarbone.

"There are so many, Lucius. So many. Take me to her, please. Please."

Sand fell down her back, then clumps of earth. Smells arose, musty, then sharper, from damp inland seas to the ozone of the ocean. The elongated shadows around her reached upward, thinning into black bars against the grey land. Then they began to slip away, reaching into the open spaces. Marcia let herself fall backward, into Lucius' painting. Water cracks.

PLAYA SONG

The hour of change. Stripes of brown and silver, a blinding white, and a grey-blue that keeps morphing. Merl lifts her head, the cracks in the dry playa floor now a red relief embedded in her cheek. Where she touches the earth there is heat, and tingling, and on her back, the sun is beginning to scorch its own pattern into her hide. The summer dress is gone, red poppies dissolved in a moment's light, only a shriveled ring of fabric around Merl's neck left behind. She pulls it free and throws it away. She needs to move. And she needs to find water.

The playa stretches ahead all the way to the distant purple-hazed mountains. Merl's arms have such trouble supporting her, each handstep so painful, desert plants pricking her palms. The wheelchair lies twisted on its side, metal fused into a new sculpture. The spokes curve into the horizon, off kilter, and the hub of the wheel has blossomed out with aluminum tongues. No one will sit on this chair anymore.

All around, the lightning strike has branded the ground. About four feet out, as far as her arms can drag her, Merl sees where the flash has marked its visit on earth. On this side, beneath her, sand has shifted into glass. On the other side, the ordinary salty sand keeps its wind and water patterns. The glass is getting hotter. She has to find a way to leave.

Her testing finger on the non-fused sand quickly retreats. Hot. And sticky, leaving grainy residue that will destroy even her callused palms much too quickly, long before Merl can crawl toward assistance.

Colored fracture lines in the glass hold the cracked patterns of the earth.

One finger, then two, insert themselves in one of the larger cracks. Merl applies pressure. A small explosion. With a 'ping' glass separates at a hair-line crack farther out. The rift in the glass moves a fraction. Merl lowers her face to the glass. She feels a cooler breath of air exhaling in an ozone-rich whiff.

The 'ping.' This is indeed real glass, and she can hear the scratches of her steel-toe boots as she shifts herself on the smooth surface.

She turns on her back. Her face to the sun high above, climbing steeply on its path, ready to burn the life out of her. She takes in a full breath, arranges herself in a pentagram on the glass, in the middle of the irregular circle fused into the desert.

She sings.

Sound breathes from her lips, first in small sips and hiccups, swelling as the mouth finds its moisture, hidden deep, and tissues lubricate with the swell of the sound.

She sings.

Sound escalates, vibrates, her monstrous wheelchair picking up the waves like an alien antenna, amplifying the sound.

She sings.

Sound mounts and bursts, her vocal cords stretching and deepening in exercise after exercise, running the scales. A small mouse, scurrying across the playa in search of a grain and shade, stops and twitches its whiskers.

She sings.

As the sun reaches its zenith high above, the sound is ready, bursting forth from burning lungs, superheated pressure shaping itself in a larynx that has survived so many toxic breaths already.

At the stroke of noon echoing across from the Wild West church steeple barely visible from the playa's flatness, the song zings its final crescendo, sustained, high, pitched to find impurities and the pressure lines that keep it all together.

The glass bursts.

The sound descends.

The singer falls.

The earth swallows and belches a spring.

Water sucks its way out of deep strata, a hydraulics of pressure geysering in the wild.

The founder of the oasis swims in languid laps and the playa blooms.

et

18 hours before the founding of the desert spring. The red sun is setting over the playa. The founder manipulates her chair wheel out of the back seat. A snap, and the yellow frame connects to the hub. Another twist, stressful on an already weak back, and the second wheel appears, held in her brown hand. She brings the complex machinery together, and the spindle of the wheel slides into the axle without a hitch.

A satisfying click and the chair is upright, balanced, a thing of rounded beauty on the hard-baked sand. She swings herself into it, closes the Prius' door, locks it, and wheels around.

The bands of the high desert lie in front of her: the border of the salt lakes, the alkaline waters shimmering in the evening heat, the layers of horizon and rising air. Birds swoop through the bands, knitting modern abstract art out of the pastel banding.

Merl releases her hands downward, gives a first hesitant push out into this wildness. The square blocks of the city are far behind, and this will be her realm, for the next four weeks, her artist residency, far away from it all.

She avoids looking at her car as she wheels forward—refuses to acknowledge the heavy scratches that have disfigured the shiny lacquer. The last sign of the urban unrest. Merl's mind is crawling toward peace, away from the screaming metal sounds that surrounded her when she had run the gauntlet out toward the 80 freeway entry off University. Her mind turns away from the people she encountered. The people at the side of the on-ramp had been bearded, some tattooed, encased in dirty Go-re-Tex or bamboo fibers. They had used scrap metal, bicycle chains or their own high-end car keys to mark her beloved Prius, as she tried to make it up onto the freeway bridge, inching her car past soft flesh and destructive metal.

Berkeley was exploding—and she rode the first shockwave out of town, long before the sidewalks were ripped up, streets blockaded, the city locked down and gnarled in place. She made it. A deep breath. The air is marked by altitude and the slight sour taste of the alkali salts floating amid the dust.

Eventually she does turn back to the scratched Prius, and, with a press of the key, the trunk opens to reveal a row of sturdy sharp-edged boxes. Whole Foods produce, her nourishment for the next four weeks. Merl's stars had shone on her, had directed her to complete her shop the day before the glint of metal began to shimmer up and down Telegraph, Shattuck and University Avenues. She had managed to snag almond butter and cans of fava beans, high-protein staples that had by now run out in all Berkeley stores.

In Lakeview, Oregon, just one hour away from her high desert residency home, she had stocked up on all perishables, yogurt, cheeses, fresh vegetables and fruit, in the dependable and slightly old-fashioned Safeway.

Merl hefts the first of the boxes out of the trunk and onto her lap. With a firm twist of her wrist, she wheels over to the cottage door. A push of her finger opens the door to her personal retreat. Coolness and raw pine wood exhale back at her. She crosses the threshold. On the other side of the patio, the playa lies wide and open.

er

24 hours before the first geysering of the desert spring. At Café Gratitude high up Berkeley's Shattuck Avenue, Carla stiffens. She is sitting in the snug corner made between the cooling

display and the bar divider, safely out of the way, not visible to anybody looking in from the street door.

Is she really safe enough? Carla can't quite parse what is going on outside, why hipsters and street citizens are on the rampage together, what the agenda is, where her own politics lie. Carla loves the Bay Area Public School, the anti-gentrification activists who make their rent by getting grants for performance art and travel the world, loves her mates at Small Press Distribution, the poets of activism and protest. So are these them, the mild graduate students, the human chain links who re-tell their stories of walking and standing with the longshoremen in Oakland's harbor, freezing the supply chains in their tracks? Or is this a different crowd, a lustier brand, swinging different kinds of chains with a jaunty air, ready to crack their Doc Martens down onto the next cockroach that tries to scuttle across the park?

Carla is bewildered, but understands that her way of grasping Berkeley's political worlds might have run its course, might have become irrelevant the moment the first bussed-in police officer's throat was cut, and a geyser of blood drenched the front window of the Himalayan restaurant down the street. The politics might have vanished an hour before this gurgling cut, alongside a wall of posters for screenings of *Fruitvale Station*, when the first five protesters found themselves astonished when another police officer's hand did not hold a nightstick, or pepper spray, but a fully loaded automatic weapon. The protesters suddenly understood the finality of the change when the officer had mowed them down, neat as a sewing machine, bullet-holes ripping apart the wooden shielding around the building site.

Carla is terrified. She had come to work this morning, has assumed that somehow, order would establish itself, that these outliers of violence would be reabsorbed into the still generally benevolent world of her youth. But no such luck. A study of post-Marxian aesthetics lays open on the bar above her head, the book still where it had been when the first stray bullet had ricocheted its way around the place. The bullet had lodged itself in a big poster, right in the curly 'g' of the "What are you grateful for?" caption. Carla isn't sure, anymore. But the time for understanding has passed. If she wants to survive, she'll have to leave this little triangle of space behind and get out of town.

She wills her legs to help her up. She only knows of one way out. The path of least people, far away from the heaving masses of Shattuck and University. Even here, inside the corridor, she can hear the screaming, sirens, helicopters and shots down the street.

She steps out through the wooden portal, past well-trimmed evergreen bushes. The street lies empty. She runs to her left, runs as fast as she can, toward Cedar Street, its mouth opening onto Shattuck just a few blocks up. She is across Telegraph, walks fast up the street, her side pressed closed to the stores that line the street. She hears a shout behind her. Unintelligible. An angry scream. She runs. The shout does not repeat, nor does the scream, and there are no running feet or roaring motors after her.

She does not let up. Finally, Cedar. She veers around the corner. The clothing store stares at her. Its window has been smashed. A mannequin bleeds out of the opening, one hand straight, pointing upward, to the place Carla is running toward: the streets out toward Tilden Park, up and out, over the hill and into the far valleys.

At least one of her skills is working for her. With the persistence of a marathon runner she jogs up, can smell the alluring aroma of Peet's coffee beans as she passes the original site of the chain store. The smell is stronger than usual. The door yawns open, and the windows have fallen out, too. A small heap of coffee beans has been thrown out onto the street, a curve of black brown pebbles creating a first stony beach bulwark, ten-

32

derly ringing their old home.

She pounds past, feels some of the outlier pebbles crack beneath her shoes.

The street begins to tilt upward, out of the coastal zone up toward the Berkeley hills. She's not even breathing hard yet. To her right, above a straggly community garden, she can see a smoke column: what could be burning and smoking like this at the corner of Center and University? She envisions an effigy of cars, their tires bleeding carbon dust back into the air. She imagines the Goodwill nearby, its doors wide open and its racks empty, old clothes fuelling a new Warpurgis day, warming the homeless folk who called a halt to their invisibility. She pictures the police, having switched allegiances, creating a circle of soil around the bonfire with spades looted from the last hardware stores clinging between the restaurants.

Carla does not wish to participate in whatever new communal festivities are arising out of the ashes out there. She runs on. Veers left, away from the action, and higher up the hill. She passes the rose garden.

The oily sheen of the Bay stretches out to her left. The sun is high now, glinting off the flatness before Mount Tamalpais ends the bay's reign. The smog is heavy in the air, a haze that just about erases the tops of the Golden Gate. And on the waters, about halfway out to the bridge, Carla sees something terrifying.

The supply chain is on fire. A giant tanker throws black dense smoke into the sky, a sacrifice, a burnt offering of the dying king drifting away from his people. Carla hears the distant pop of the superheated containers, their sides curving out like lilies, innards spilling into the slick-covered waters below. She imagines electronics, children's bicycles, sunglasses, all floating then sinking out of sight and, finally, the demise of an old Ferrari that had made its way all the way from Italy, never to roar to life again, a long ship journey only to be vanquished, to drown in a deep underwater canyon.

Carla stands for a minute, gives her calves a rest. No one is around, the air is deadly still. She reaches out, snaps off a pink and white rose, and inhales.

er

The girl is going to get away, and Jim is not ok with that. Uh-Huh. No way, little bitch. There is too much going on down University, the city is in flames, and if you get too close, you will get fucking burned. Oh yes, he is not stupid. This here, though, nice and tender, ready for the plucking, roses and all.

Jim likes roses: he remembers roses in the band tattoos emblazoned on Kevin's walls, his older brother's pad, deep down in the dungeon of their Ohio paradise. He and his brother had dragged their racing gear all over their non-existing town center, sticking it to the police man, swinging in the wind. Roses, and heavy bass, and tinkering with washed-out family cars till they hang like low-riders and boomed through town.

Kevin didn't make it out of Ohio. His ass got kicked one night in a drag race, the revved up Mazda folded into a hunk of metal and plastic stuffing. And right in there, Kevin.

Jim had stood by the side of the Mazda, could see some of his spray paint patches, not quite as accomplished as Kevin's. He could see his brother's head, resting on what remained of the steering wheel. He can still remember the muscular arm across his own breastbone, Howard, one of Kevin's mates, dragging him backward, away from the car. He still hears the sound of his sneakers on the rough asphalt, half-carted away, remembers the weave in Howard's old jean jacket. He still smells the stink of hot gas one tick before he sees Kevin's hair go up around his head in a halo of fire, the head jerking upright for one final time, as if he is alive—was he alive? And then the car rocks back on its heels and yowls with the fire searing through its heart.

Jim's Keds got all scratched up, fouled by road dust, heat, and the mud by the side of the road. He still wears them, right now, long past their preppy shine and into the deeper rock-n-roll, sneaking up on little Miss Sunshine with the rose in her hand.

Carla holds the rose between thumb and forefinger, carefully, attending to her beating heart, stilling it, like her coaches have taught her. Her head snaps to the left, sensing movement. Blond dreadlock boy is coming up sideways, coming at her like a crab, scurrying across the street. Grey sweatshirt with hoodie, cigarette slim jeans, half street kid, half street cool. Not exactly threatening, not on a normal fine day, not with the flow of the city around them. But today, in the middle of riots, fancy homes up on the hill with shut faces and turned away eyes? A different story. Not an ending she wants to wait for. She inhales the rose's perfume, tosses the flower, and picks up her speed again. A few vast sprints put her well out of reach of the crab, even as he abandons all nonchalance and lunges for her.

"Bitch!" he screams, and she, normally well terrified by confrontation, bellows back.

"Wanker!" A deep and satisfying vibration of her diaphragm.

ℰ𝓇

22 hours to the founding of the new desert oasis. Howard drives on, unperturbed. His wheels, a gallon bottle of water next to his seat, two big bags of Doritos, and two six-packs tucked away in the cooler in the bed of the pick-up. He had left the landscaping job in Oakland's Lake Merritt Park right on the dot, at 2pm, shift change. Till then he'd been in his usual haze, picking up and packing out garbage all morning long, ears and eyes closed to all else. But it hadn't been easy: life on the waterfront had been quite a bit more hectic than usual, what with

screaming sirens and joyriders flooring and wrecking cars all about, with lots of people running, not for fun or stamina, but with fear and abandon. He'd seen someone with a monitor in his arms, obviously looted. And when he did straighten, looked toward the horizon, he had seen a plume of black smoke, from somewhere near Broadway. Huh.

On the stroke of two he had put away his tools. There wouldn't be cash for him, he knew, and he was a bit doubtful if the city's check would come through this time. He contemplated driving over to his digs, but, his ears full of the siren's wail, he decided against it. He climbed in, hands on his steering wheel, and nosed her out and up, back streets to the road over the hill, ready to plunge down near Orinda. Time to get out.

At the turn-off to Tilden Park, he surprised himself by braking for a hitch-hiker. She was good looking, sure, but he wasn't that kind of man, and she had also looked frightened and strong. Not a bad combination. He could tell that she had run far, seen her calf muscles bulging and the sweat outlining her arms and neck. Mousy white woman, but steely, in her own way.

"Where to?"

"Just out of here. I just came up from Berkeley. It's dangerous out there."

"Okay. Buckle up, and here we go. Direction outta here."

They had talked just a little bit, after the first fifteen minutes saw them safely past Walnut Creek, and onto the road to the Martinez Bridge. Fifteen minutes of companionable silence, and of the concentration needed to make it past a herd of fleeing cars, keeping the pickup lined up and ready.

So here they are, rolling. The bridge, and then the turn-off to Vacaville. Past the prison exits. Howard avoids looking at the exit sign, floors the accelerator a bit. He knows people in there, a hot hellhole. He's escaping.

Carla, that's her name. She talks, after a while.

Nervous chatting, for a bit, was it this or that that started the riots, who is right, protesters, tax payers, police. Whatever. He does not give a damn, and soon she picks up on it and lets it go.

"I am thinking Oregon. Up the 5, clear ride, then over at Mount Shasta."

"I haven't been there. Sounds good. We'll need liquids, I imagine, and some food."

"I have some sleeping bags and pads in the back. We'll be ok with them. And I'll stop at a Walmart once we are on the 5. Do you have some cash?"

"I have my credit card with me."

"And you got credit?"

She looks at him, uncomprehending at first. Then it dawns.

"Yes. Good limit. Unless they stop credit altogether."

"We better make it to a Walmart fast."

And they do. Out here, life looks normal. No TV in sight, and the store is well stocked. They grab two trolleys, fill them up, food and drink and mosquito spray. Howard wishes he'd grabbed a can from his job. But that's not his way, and Carla seems undisturbed by the prices. She pays. They tank up. On-ward.

Past Redding the road thins. They are now on the 299. To their left, Mount Shasta stands solid and protective. Howard loves riding under her: he feels the presence and is reassured. His shoulders drop some more, and he rolls down the window, letting in the heat. His arm hooked over the door, he stretches and the creases in his neck loosen.

"God's own country."

"Militia's own country."

"Welcome off the grid, baby."

"Shall we put the radio on?"

She is getting really nervous now, he can see her twitching in her seat.

They try, for a while, catch relatively little. NPR has a story:

riots in the Bay Area, hot spot Berkeley, disturbances in SF and Oakland, short segment, little new info. They feel a bit silly, but then each remembers glimpses of what they saw: Howard, a young girl with a cut on her face, dragged behind a grown man carrying nothing but a big water bottle. Carla, the eyes of the crab by the rose garden, the sly assault.

They turn the radio off. No conversation. They drive, eyes strafing by giant trees and giant mountains, gophers daring to cross the road in a flash of fast living.

Early evening. Howard turns off the road. Pit River campground.

"Nice place, pretty small. Not many likely to be around. Good?"

The first words uttered in over an hour. She nods. There's a whole roadful of emotions swarming over her face as he's slowing down, and he can see that. She's thinking.

He's not, not really: the rocks and the trees, and the squirrels and the sun is all he needs. But when one looks up, stuff happens. So he feels some sadness for this young woman by his side, her insides twisting in wild filmstrips only she can see.

He wants to tell her about stillness and just looking, but he can't find the words. All he can do is save her, bring her to the river with him, and offer quiet by the rushing water.

er

18 hours to the geysering. Howard and Carla drive around the campground at the bottom of the valley that the Pit River, the Achuma, has cut for itself. Large trees and the constant roar of the white water fill their eyes and ears.

They are not quite alone. Two large Campervans share the grounds and three dome tents peek out from other bays. But there is space for them and they back the pick-up truck up one of the gravel spurs. Howard unrolls a pad and a sack for himself. Carla decides to stay in the truck bed, an arrangement that works fine for them both.

Soon they sit by the rushing river, drinking Diet Dr. Pepper out of cans, and gnawing on peanut butter sandwiches assembled with Howard's pocket knife.

"Where are you driving to, do you know?" Carla asks.

"There's a place in Oregon, high desert country, by the alkali lakes. There's a campground there, far away from people, but with reliable water. And hot springs. It'll be good."

She nods. Sounds good, as good as any. What they had heard on the radio didn't sound good at all. Too many weapons, protests, the National Army in the Bay Area, and she had heard about fires at the Lawrence Livermore National Laboratory.

Carla is exhausted. Howard is silent, though he wants to talk, wants so desperately to talk to her, to tell her, to make her see why it is becoming so important to him to keep her safe. He turns, but he can feel her keeping her distance, that she can feel his urgency and that it makes her shrink. He retreats, turtling his neck and swiveling away. He plants his feet inches from the waterline. He eats.

The water calms him. He dozes.

His mind glides over accidents, explosions, the fiery scorch of his past. Kevin going up in a glory of fire, a Phoenix in Ohio. His arms hold Kevin's little brother close, a heart beating next to his own.

Two years later, another crash, on the turnpike. Howard's van lies twisted and grotesque in the far lane, a broken mammoth with a crushed Volvo in its mouth. There will be fire soon, and this time, the figure in his arms is a young woman, unknown, unknowable, her face black with soot and slack with shock. She isn't blistered, has survived the whoosh of the fire drumming the sky, but her figure is strangely lax in his arms. Something is terribly wrong. Ambulances, hospital eventually, insurance agents. All is taken care of. He has never seen her again. And now, with the smell of turpentine and smog still in his clothes, there they are, white and drifting on the river: the flowers he has trampled, floating.

Carla knows nothing of these dreams. She wants to run, to find the horizon. This glade and the rushing river's noise enclose her, and she startles with each shiver in the bushes. She has tried a few times to ring friends in the Bay but no call goes through. Her mobile is useless now, her world shrunken to a peanut butter jar and the knife, to her muscles and her ability to focus. She hugs herself hard, the sinews and long muscles of her torso warm and taut against her skin.

"Goodbye." She whispers to her mum, her dad, her friends, after Howard has turned in for the night and left her alone by the rushing river. She crouches, her mobile in her hand, open and lit. She creates a little nest of sticks, a raft, to hold the phone in the smoother waters near the rushes. It sails off, a little lit rectangle in the falling night, bobbing from time to time. Carla can't see if it turns a corner in the river or drowns.

et

6 hours before the song ruptures the playa. Howard awakes, rolls out of his dreams of scorching fire, his throat aflame, screaming and caught in the folds of his sleeping bag. In a second, Carla is off the truck and by his side.

Howard keens, still half asleep, and Carla holds him, rocking him.

They sit and rock, the world shifting beneath and above them into morning. Stars fade slowly, and a green gold glow creeps over the horizon.

The keening stops, and Carla feels Howard's muscles uncramp, relax, fall heavily toward earth. His face is blank and the eyes won't look at her. She withdraws her arms and they sit side by side on the sleeping pad, looking out at the green walls around them.

Something small rotates into view, a shadow against the slowly vibrating leaves on the bushes. They both stare. Another move, an angular twist of an articulated leg, down, over, up. A small lizard emerges, a salamander, black with yellow spots as if bees' wax has dripped from an old alchemist's table. The salamander moves across the clearing, stays off the sharper grit that surrounds the tent site. It stops. Maybe it detects their heartbeat, or their thermal signature. Frozen in the air, only the eyes and tongue move, a small pendulum. Howard and Carla are measured. The rising sun's rose sky reflects in the silvery coils of the salamander's eyes. The creature moves on, toward the sounds of the river.

It is time to pack and get on the road again. The truck is readied in minutes. Howard and Carla step down to the river for a few minutes, their ears full with the rushing and falling of water. Then they climb in, Howard with the achy morning hitch that dropped into his bones so many years ago, that night in the van, breathing petrol fumes into a woman's life; Carla, nimble, holding on the overhead struts of the truck as she swings herself into place. Next stop, past the green and blue, into the banded lands: Oregon's alkali lakes. Behind them the skies begin to change.

$\mathcal{e\tau}$

An hour after the emergence. The founder arcs her back, her legs a sea anemone beneath her, beside her, floating white in the blue. She has tried to crawl onto the land, but the new lake's edges are sculpted glass, bulbous forms with sharp edges. Merl does not want to cut unknowingly into unfeeling flesh. The water is warm, thermal, but not scalding or unpleasant. It is drinkable, tastes delicious and health-giving, with an edge of metal. The mineral content makes her float easily, and she

41

watches hair and limbs entwine around her, delights in sensual rolls and curves, her strong arms carving furrows through the water.

Merl sings to herself, not the keening of the rupture but a pleasant vocalization, old melodies and newer harmonies melding on her tongue. The sun is high above her, and she can no longer hear the church bells, or any sounds. Only the water lapping at the glass rim.

Later, change.

Two heads appear above her. Merl is nearly transparent now, her tissues swelled and full with the desert water. The heads talk. She tries to focus her thoughts to decode the sounds. She raises a hand, a greeting, a blessing, an invitation. The heads withdraw. Merl sings.

Later still. A new sight. A raft is lowered into her lake. Antlers and sticks make a filigree nest, old amazon book box air cushions provide lift, and, in the raft, jars of peanut butter, white bread, and packets of beef jerky stand in neat rows, surrounded by nutritional bars and small sealable containers with toilet paper tissue. Merl sings to the raft.

Larger sounds. A wave. One being has jumped in and she is no longer alone. After a while, the second. The beings are naked like her, light and dark brown sinuous shapes darting around her. She does not wish to stop singing, and there is nothing to say.

They all touch and drift. The sky changes color above them now, pearlescent shades bow to a deep red, then a white flash. The air moves. They float.

DUMPLING'S PILLAR

That day I had dropped off my refrigerated messenger bag at the food coop after my last bike run. It was such a heavy thing and however I padded the strap it chafed the spot between my breasts and the edge of my neck. Sheila, my fellow food runner, had stared down at her phone.

"Toni, look. What's on the board is weird. It's not coming up here."

We had looked together, each of us locked into our little screen jewels, hers bright pink with lurid violet stripes, like the chevrons on her biking pants. My own phone was a bit older, grey, with fine asphalt dots, quite heavy in my pudgy hand. I needed to upgrade.

The list on the screen looked too familiar: this was the route I had tracked earlier that day. All these lunches had already been delivered by my achy calves, my wheels clasping the street as I pumped myself along. But here the addresses refused to go away, their map icons crowding the screen. I had shrugged, even though I would have loved to have been able to help Sheila of the silky hair. But there was nothing I could do, and she was getting frustrated. I left her pressing buttons, refreshing the picture.

My lonely weekend began. At the station I locked my bike carefully, after choosing rack mates comparable in prize and age, so as to not attract looters.

People everywhere. All waiting. When I took out my ear buds I heard the announcement, first in Norwegian, then in English. All the trains in Southern Norway were down, standing still, their massive engines cooling in the early fall sunshine. And that included my scenic ride to Bergen, over the mountains and through the troll passes, past glaciers and pewter-colored lakes that drown all memory.

There was no outcry. In Oslo station the tour groups stood a bit forlorn, waiting to be told which track to go to for the replacement bus. They waited for an hour, then slowly dispersed, some to hunt in the labyrinth for a bus, some to go back to their hotels, to see if there was still a bed there for the night ahead. I watched the tourists, sitting on my soft bag, with all my e-gear safely tucked in the middle, juicing my phone. It turned out that I would not use most of the chargers much longer. Soon, most would be garlands in old Christmas trees, slung like off-white offal into the green plastic branches.

That night I just watched. The station speakers would crackle on, ever so often, informing us that all trains were standing still, encouraging us to search for alternative transportation routes. I had nowhere particular to be. I was able to tap into the web for a bit longer, checked Facebook, looked for weekend emails, missives from far away.

"I am thinking of you."

Nothing much appeared, and Facebook was a screaming riot of US election coverage. I clicked away the page. I would not see it again.

At one point, early in the night, I went outside to stretch my legs. I walked past a city planting full of blue and purple violets. The flowers shivered in the black soil. I leaned over the bed and heard the gurgle of the water spouts beneath the earth. The water flowed, bubbled, growled, and the roots danced in the pressure waves. Soon they'd drown completely. Normally a signal would tell the wider system of the malfunctioning water cut-off. But tonight the water flushed on in never-ending spurts and the violets moved in a last dance.

Alternatives. We were running out now, you see. Those communication nodes that broke in the food map apps, then the trains—these were advance warning, canaries, but we didn't see it at the time. Instead we made jokes about Norwegian trolls and underground destruction squads. But the spark that laid low the trains and watering systems and underground and bus arrival times, that spark or worm or virus crawled its way into the wider waves, too. Two days after the dancing flowers, the internet went dark.

So there I was, in the dark. Watching. I could not report on my nightly migrations on Facebook. I had nobody to tell my stories to. All that was left were tiny blips of connectivity. Local phone-to-phone chains. Decentralized, eroding and low-grade.

From that point on, when I took my charged phone out, I learned to look for a different little icon, a stylized phone rather than the bar fan. And if I saw it, I could hunt for the password. It might be hidden in a graffiti tag, plastered like chewing gum on a wastepaper basket, or written each new hour in chalk on the damp pavement. Somewhere, the magical list of numbers and letters would jumble out at the diligent searcher. Then I could reach my hand into a new thicket of electronic tracks, get a little touch crack. I could post a low-res image, or a snippet of text. Someone nearby, in the same wi-fi web, might reply. We each might look around, see if someone else was typing. These phone nets were very local. The old anonymity of the web was gone, but a new stranger contact world was being born, right here.

Let's go hunting, my friend. Let's go and search for connection.

The evening was drawing down, filaments of smoke and exhalation shifted in color bands over the fjord. The opera house still gleamed prismatic on the harbor. Next to it, the crumpled steel and glass flame in the water was hung with the debris of a new world: mobile phones, hung on their charger strings across the glistening facets, like drippy mourning stones, or black spaghetti.

I still held on to my phone, of course, my access point to the low-fi world.

There was Kristin. I recognized her coming out of our favorite Ethiopian at Gronland Station. Some restaurants were still working, while supply chains trundled out and the warehouses got depleted. People kept warning about food shortages. As a food messenger, I knew how quick the balance could shift, out back, in the kitchens, with empty fridges, empty bags, all in the blink of an eye. But there was a good stock of lentils, and while the menu was getting smaller, we were not in the cellar yet.

Kristin jogged over, her cool fingers wrapped around the take-out container with its injera, hot lentils and Berbere sauce. She usually shared, if I wheedled up to her just right. I had bartering goods, too, fried onions, some sausage ends, from the Turkish baker in my neighborhood. There were still neighborhoods, even though most of the tourists trapped in Oslo roamed the streets at night.

Between the two of us we had a full meal. We greeted each other, our take-out containers held at an angle, intentions clear, no threat. Like urban dogs on two legs, we ran through the protocol. Our little habits had already become quite ingrained, only a few weeks after the catastrophe. It did not take long for safety rituals to assert themselves, and us women were always good at working out fast solutions. After the circling, she initiated, took off her outermost jacket, and placed it on the ground. Like an old-school picnic blanket, but more dusty, army-green, like urban paint warfare scenes. We were Mad Max survivors. But in the end, we both managed to sit down next to one another, and opened our cartons, and shared the food.

Kristin was the blonde leggy one to my small dark dumpling. No boobs to speak of, but hair like sunshine, and violet eyes. Really violet, like vampires and werewolves. I would have given her my blood, but she had not asked for it. She was funny, too, and hard-core. Edgy, otherwise she would have hung her mobile on the harbor sculpture, too, and joined the wailing.

Remember when we were all into Pokemon Go? Competition for gym dominance, elaborate dragons at our beck and call? She had that edge, the look that meant that she's sizing up what to take on, at what to throw the ball.

I was not that much to look at. Short legs, stubby arms, torso too long for my arms. No waist at all, hip tires enough to outfit a Jeep. But I had my own edge. I soldiered, marched, shifted forward in tanker mode, whatever you did to me, whatever dyke names you threw my way. All systems go, and it was hard to stop me marching once I was on the move. So in some ways I could see why Kristin hooked up with me at nights, to share food and go wi-fi-ing together in sketchy neighborhoods. I didn't think any of us would live very long. So we made it count, blonde sweets and chocolate tank.

We ate the lentils with elegant handfuls of sour bread. Likewise, the onions and sausage ends. It was filling, and I loved the feeling of injera in my right hand, the way it stuck gently to my fingertips, a soft warm caress. There I was again, munching and dreaming. Kristin knew it of course, and ribbed me, teased me with her side-eye and eyelashes. I knew we both loved it.

Time to cruise. We clicked open our phones, screen lights turned way low to preserve the juice. We still had plenty of electricity in Oslo, but we'd heard about lights out in the far country, whole swathes of country going dark at curfew. We were good at this. But what we did drained the phones, and we wanted to keep at it for a few hours, at least, without having to suck at the e-teat. Also, dimmer was safer. We did not know who exactly was out hunting at night, hunting for more than poetry snippets.

Kristin found it first—a well, a wide open network. "Lana Net" was the name that came up, and the name whispered old movies and shapely hips in its swing. A few minutes of hunting about, and I found the entry code. It was stenciled small and tight into the neckline of a plunging bosom painted on the old roller-skating ring. Two boobs, no head, just a Victoria's Secret tight stack. The numbers and letters were in the white lace edging the blue bra. Nice one.

We hooked in. Flash. A stream gurgled into my Samsung, her iPhone. This was an active hole, a full well of sensation. We took turns reading out what scrolled over the tiny screens.

"Touch me now."

"Your feathers are silky tonight, my dove."

"I am in Venice, velvet mask pressed to my skin, patchouli."

"I am looking for Daliah. 5'10", dark skin, tattoo of a night-lily on her left biceps. Seen?"

"See the pillar rising."

"See the pillar rising."

"I see the pillar."

"Be my altar, pillar."

Ok, there seemed to be a theme here. Kristin and I agreed to look for the pillar. What could that be, around here? We were in a spacious concrete neighborhood, the back alley of tourist stores near the city center train station. Some trash containers on the left. The skater ring straight ahead. An avenue of city trees to our right, angling away from us. Was that a likely site for worshipping pillars? We investigated in that direction.

This was not as easy as it sounds. The park angled beneath the city surface. It was built into the hillside. We'd had to go down, and it was dark in there. In the before-time, street folk assembled around there. In the center of the park was a spoke of meeting lanes and a circular bench. Not an easy or safe space for women to go hunting for pillars at night. But the rules had changed. Leaves crunched under our boots as we descended the slope, phones in hand. Where was this pillar?

Soon, we were at the central circular space. Leaves had drifted into patterns, herringbones over paving stones. Many of the city buildings around us were dark at night. Windows grinned at us with Halloween teeth. It was not quite pitch dark, but we knew that those street lights might not come up again. The leaves rustled beneath our feet. We couldn't see anybody around: not homeless, not player.

We stood in the circle, backs to each other, turning clockwise, scanning. There. The messages seemed to load quicker to the West. We moved that way, eyes half on the screen, half on the path ahead. The trees around us were coppiced, and bulbous gnarls had bled their strength into wooden canker fists. We nodded to each other—these were pillars more than trees. This was it. We moved closer. Kristin palpated the bark of one of the old ones. Rough, map tracks she couldn't quite read, like a blown-up fingerprint. She shook her head, moved on. I hung back a bit, tried to keep an eye out for company. Then, she beckoned me closer.

"Dumpling, look at this."

Did I mention that she had a strange sense of affection? I joined her by the twisted tree stump. She took my hand. I tingled all over, but let her guide my hand to where she wanted to go. She smirked at me.

Then I touched it.

It was warm, glowing in the tree's old stone feel. We each traced the bark area with our fingers, and found a big circle. As clear an invitation as any. This was the pillar. And somewhere behind that, there was a party.

We sat down for a bit, checked the traffic. It had gone steamy fast.

"I lick the salt."

"I lick the pepper."

"I lick strawberries on the young masqueur's belly."

"Let me pepper you, alright."

"Flowers of clove buds, my darling."

"Salt lattice, to chain you on."

"Sugar crystals to rub into your wounds."

Kristin was intrigued, I could see it. She liked the baroque ones, the scene play, remnants of the cosplayers we each had observer-stalked in Vinland Park on weekends. We had told each other this as secrets, marking our bond. Now it was coming back to bite me.

She really wanted to go in. I tried to reason with her. Got nowhere. Because where was there to go when we both knew that food would run out soon, and that it was all doomed, anyway?

"You have to let it come to you."

Ok. Sure. I tried to tune in. She was good at this. I could see the little blue veins in her small hand. That's how blonde she was. The hand rested against the warm tree circle, touching, stroking, and I could feel it. Full on. I hoped the tree had a good time.

It seemed that it did. The warm circle receded, shifted into the tree stump. Kristin stepped closer to the tree and bent forward, into the open hole. I could have screamed with terror. But I did not. Instead, I crowded near, as I couldn't imagine my stroking hands having the same effect on the tree. So I made sure to ride Kristin's coattails. I put my hands on where her coattails would be, got an impatient swish for my efforts. But also a giggle. Good.

She pushed herself up some more and glided in. I just went and did the same stupid thing. Up, over, down. We were belly-down, riding a smooth wood tube. If I had been three years younger, I likely would have been screaming with laughter. Instead, I was terrified. But she was up ahead, and she was banking, using her arms and hands to align in the tunnel, to twist up or down with the turns. I had no idea how deep we were, but we were riding this.

A bump. She was out. I was out. We were in a feather bed. Or something duvet-like, comfortable, warm, soft. We each scrambled out of the way, off, for it was also pitch black down here. Where were we? I reached for Kristin's hand. She did not withdraw it, and our fingers interlinked. It was electric, pink fire, velvet.

We pulled out our phones. Dialed up the light a little bit.

Now they were flashlights, too. The Lana conversation was hot and heavy, and flew across our screens, like a randy chat-room scene, but more stilted, no swearwords, heavy on the romantic. Old emo, maybe. Who were these dudes or dudettes?

We rounded a bend in the tunnel. Now we could see light. Straight ahead. It was hard to see what it was. There were refractions, shimmerings, mirrors in mirrors. There was a lake down there, and a crystal island, and a crystal forest, and a disco ball ruled over it. Candle light, at least that's what it looked like to me then, flickering and unsteady. The light was caught and thrown into the water, shifted into the lattices of quartz crystals, jewel lights and watery wavy reflections against white limestone. It was like a ballroom down there.

Kristin was enchanted. We tucked our phones away and approached. There were figures. As we got near, they became clearer, three, no, four, one higher up on the shore of this cave lake, three on the island. They stood still, but they looked like sprung coils, ready to bolt. They were wary. Kristin did not care.

"Lana Tribe!"

She sang out. I tried to hush her, to play it down a bit. I could imagine so many scenarios in which this was a bad idea. She did not look back, rushed down. My hand was still entwined with hers, so I followed.

The dude on the shore of the cave lake seemed cool. Queer, I got the vibe strong and clear. I relaxed far in my backbone. He was family, brown skin, black hair, pomade, hipster outfit circa 1970 reimagined as urban chic. He smiled at exuberant Kristin.

"Welcome to the Lana Tribe!" He shouted, his frequency similar to Kristin's, just one octave lower. They were full of glee, the two, like brother and sister at play.

I tried to look over to the lake island, to the three figures there, but I was having a hard time seeing them clearly. Who were they? What were they? Glee dude told us he was the ferryman, and to step right in. He handed over cushions, too.

"Get comfy, kids, I'll get you over!"

We stepped in. His hand was out, and it felt like really bad karma not to cross his palm. Whatever that meant. I dug deep in my pockets, and found a few sausage links from the Turkish baker. I arced a querying eyebrow. Would that do? That would do. He seemed well satisfied. We settled, and he poled the boat into the lake and toward the center island.

Soon, we had covered the distance. The water lapped black at the boat, but the walls kept throwing light at us, skipping over the waves we were creating as our craft zipped forward. The island was really close now. It was made out of large quartz crystals, all sharp edges and mirror surfaces, octagons and long lances of white. I was not sure how one could step onto these without slipping, and I really did not want to slip into these black waters. All the light stopped short down there, and no hint of what lay below escaped the surface.

Then, a small bump. We had arrived. Our guide hadn't said a word the whole time he'd been punting us over, and he was silent now, all glee now coiled. His eyes showed the way—over there, over the white expanse of sharp broken edges. Over to the three shapes, still indistinct.

The people there freaked me out. Was that fur on their bodies? Why was there this halo all around them? Where were the others? The wi-fi traffic was intense, and yet none of these people seemed to be working on phones. They were just standing there. No. Now they were turning, like one, turning to face us. I knew I did not want to see them straight on.

I tried to step back, but there was Kristin, of course, pulling on my arm, nearly pulling the sleeve off me in her eagerness to get there, to connect. I tried to get her attention, to comment on the freaky scene that was going on, but she just galloped over the sharp translucent landscape, up and over to the three silent figures.

I followed as best as I could without twisting my ankles. We arrived. The crystal forest became a pebbled circle here, small round quartz stones of all hues, lavender for amethyst, yellow for citrine, all dusky and shaded in the half-light of the cave. Where was the light coming from? The figures in the center of the circle seemed to be lit themselves. I could see them better now.

That was not fur all over them, neither was it a halo. It was light-emitting, and bristly. It reminded me of the old toys of my childhood: fiber optic half-globes, glowing in all colors and twirling. That's what these people looked like, as if tiny bristles of fiberglass stuck out of them, all over, prismatic lights at the edges, shining outward. It was mesmerizing, and the closer we came, the more amazing the colors glowed, twirled, ran over them like furry caterpillars.

Beneath the fur, the figures were pastel. I could see a face green as if a disco diva had dusted it down with her eyeshadow. Another brow looked purple, over there, a red hand, gleaming under the light bristles. They were androgynous, hairless apart from the bristles; mixed black, white, Asian; with strange twistings in their fingers, and long ropy bands over their forearms like scarification tattoos. I thought of lava lamps. I might have said that out loud: Kristin pushed me gently, as if admonishing me. I shut up.

"Are you the Lana tribe?"

Really? That was Kristin's first question? Here we were, finding some strange alien human creatures under the earth, on a crystal lake, and she asked questions like a Survivor castaway. I tried to chuckle, but the sound stuck in my craw. Kristin's question echoed over the lake, asked again and again, her voice shifting pitch as the crystals around us vibrated as if in answer.

No sound from the strange ones. Or was there? Kristin hushed me. I was not making a sound anyway. The echo died down, eventually, but there was a tone in the air now like a hum or a bell. The tone did not die, but rose shimmering like the light in the cave, rose again, got bigger rather than louder, and then it was in my head, and I was not sure if I was hearing with my ears or my teeth, my bones, my sinuses.

Wow. Ok. Enough. I could see Kristin suffering next to me, not sure where to put her hands to block the escalating sound-wave. Then it was over. Quiet.

A gentle fall of drops somewhere in the cave, so loud in the hollow left by the departing crystal wave. Some strange chit-terings. Mice? Spiders? I thought spiders, probably the thing that could scare me most down here, big furry hard-carapaced spiders with eight eyes staring at me.

The three light folks shifted position in the crystal ball cir-cle, and now I could see where the chittering was coming from. It had probably been there the whole time, but our ears had needed a tune-up to hear it. It was a familiar sound, actually. Behind the light people, ten or so crystals reached high up, like beams, or prison bars. White, translucent, terribly sharp at the edges. These were the pillars. Behind the crystal pillars, I could see a bunch of youngsters, just like Kristin and me, kids with parkas and colorful leggings, some with wrapped feet, some with sneakers, all typing away at their phones. This was the Lana tribe. Not the light creatures with their fiber optic fur.

Down there, in the cave that did not freeze, in the blood-let-ting of the crystal grid, this tribe stayed in their gym, their cas-tle, their stronghold. Long wires looped from the phones to the crystal pillars. The wires were not black, like the chargers that looped at the opera house. These were white, virginal white, much whiter than Apple's charging cords. Blindingly white, glowing milk lapping out of the matrix into the machines.

The kids were typing, their fingers glowing rosy and ma-roon, depending on skin color, little dots of red-tinged light hovering over the tiny screens. They sat hunched beyond the crystal pillars. Backs shaped into Cs, into coils of spine power.

The shoulders were relaxed, the heads bowed, drowsing. They seemed asleep, even, only fingertips awake to the juice. Maybe their eyeballs shifted with the changing charts and images on the screen. The chittering was the sound of their typing.

I did not want to see their eyeballs, I realized. I really did not want to get closer, did not want to jack into the pillar milk. So I pulled on Kristin, again. She stood still, for a sec, but then she leaned forward, poised like a greyhound before the race.

She was so beautiful then, my shimmery rose one. So tender. I felt the skin on the top of her hand. Smooth and soft, freckles of summer sun still on the white flesh. I was crying. She turned one last time. Her hand came up to my face, touched my round red cheek, a goodbye in her eyes. This was the place of the soft laser-fighting ones, connected, milky sweet flow, hard on the keyboard, integrated spines. She would soon be hooking in there, between the crystals, before the food fights began, up-stairs, above the cave, in the city. She was not crying. This was home for her.

I had delivered her here, safely, and that was my part of the story. I was the dumpling looking for remnants of Turkish food while there were still some trucks that shuttled back and forth. I would find a way to make a campfire. No doubt I would find a bunch of others, greasy hair low over our brows, to defend against rat hordes and human gangs. She was already lost to me. Kristin stepped away like a crane, into the white.

Punt boy whistled behind me. It was time to leave.

Dinosaur Dreams

Tomorrow Melanie will fly off to her new college. All will be new. She dreams.

It's the dream of the forest of quadruped giant legs. Wrinkled, in dark colors, the legs march, majestic. She sees one wrinkled mass, a muscle contracted, skin in folds shifting against the backdrop of another giant pulsing piston.

She realizes she is tiny, a dewdrop, clinging on. A tiny-ness beyond words, her eyes too small to take in these dinosaur legs articulating against one another with each long stride.

Earth is a round marble on the edge of a hair's hair. Deep in her dream, she feels the infinite smallness of her home, and herself. Every time the dream comes to her the smallness constricts her throat, her torso, breath barely escaping. These dinosaur legs are too big to notice her existence, earth too small to warrant a brush. So small that even touch would not dislodge the round planet, so small that it would pass between molecules, hovering without gravity, held by frictional affinities. Earth is insignificant. It will not matter. The legs will piston on, and Earth is gone or not, oxygen or ozone, radiant or radiated. It has no bearing on the course of the big creature striving toward something she can't hold in her mind.

The dream contracts again. Melanie's hip distances itself from her collarbone. Small displacement. A vertebra nudges itself toward the left. A lung alveolus twists out of place into the new hollow released by the bone's curve. A hair's breath's shift. Yet Melanie's respiration charges through her chest, unfamiliar territory opening under her pelvis.

She remembers the time her dentist left a ridge on a tooth's filling, shifting her bite. She had been in agony for weeks, trying to adjust to the new slivery reality of this jawbone's articulation against the skull. She hadn't been able to and had to go back, ask them to file down the barely noticeable edge, embarrassed by the side eye of the dentist.

Now here on her bed, she can feel the energy leaking out of her right side, the kink of dream torsion deflating the internal balloon between hip and shoulder. In her half-sleep Melanie is close to weeping. Hates sensitivity, her inner space rigidity. The single tear, when it tracks loose from the eyelash, is lava on her cheek. Salts burn epithelial cells.

Near dawn Melanie shifts, volcanic terror at her core. Then, a cool web drapes over the sensations, pulls down, and cradles her into sleep.

ex

The assassin waits for his target, lets the motor idle cool as an air-conditioned cat at the foot crossing, rivers of people gushing out of department stores and fast-food joints, hip-hugging bags clutched to sweaty bodies long overdue for a sit-down, sundown, a space of rest unburdened by Monday mornings.

ex

Akilah walks along the street.

Never oblivious, never just stepping, her feet mark the hot pavement, a faint indentation of her heel remains in the tar. Akilah's hair magnetizes the gaze of the white man on the scaffold, the white man in the subway station, the white woman at the coffee store.

ex

Across the well-travelled road, the assassin marks the woman named Akilah, compares her to the photo in the folder. Hair, posture, the tilt of the neck. Yes.

He rolls into traffic, carefully, slowly creeping, like a tourist ready to be unpredictable, unclear, lost in the big city.

❧

Akilah cannot demagnetize her hair, drape it casually, thrown into the wind. She remembers other spaces. She remembers home space, family space, a diaspora she reaches toward, where the cut of her cloth or the pattern of the skirt mark her, not the hue of her skin, the flap over chastised bones. She walks.

❧

His foot descends, clutch into gear, shift space, forward motion glued to his victim's retreating back. Akilah arrows, and he can see that she has not a care in the world, bone certainty about her goal and her destination: the next protest action, standing in the wave of white and standing proud.

❧

Akilah walks, forty years and counting, walking the ruins of slavery's game. She does not look anybody in the eye. Cattle calls of city center, she despises the easy money easy clothes of the whore brides, the fat barons that trample the pavement into uniformity.

❧

The assassin in his car is nearly level with Akilah now, the game thinning, his game sure as he slides the gun out of the shoulder holster, its fine calf honed to the softness of an inner thigh. He does not know how often he fingers it, deep beneath his clavicle, his buffalo refuge, veldt certainty of the side his fingers are on. It's a tell, and he had to work to control and suppress the urge, the fingering, now only in free flow when he knows himself to be alone. Or just before he kills.

ℰ

Akilah moves eel-like now, a clot of people stopping the road, cuing for theater admittance for the Saturday matinee. Her shoulders slope past ermine, white softness with a deadly odor. Shimmering sequins, high-hipped on high heels. Here, Akilah enjoys the press, the give, the weft of her dreadlocks swishing over velvet, her own sharp short blazer cutting into a common cloth. Fish weave, water flow.

ℰ

He has not lost his target, follows easily along in the street, through the throng of people in front of the theatre. Akilah's high coiffure, knot upright, one lance of lock sticking straight, points the way. The gun's plastic in his hand is warm, smooth. Check.

ℰ

Akilah exits the crowd, her hips shimmy from the warm human sea. This is home, too: the easy weave in a sea of excitement, anonymous fish swish. Alone, now, forward.

ℰ

The assassin is pulling level, the street emptier now, soon, soon.

⹑

Akilah has escaped the policemen in the riot, in the car check, at the protest's borders. "Are you carrying a gun, ma'am?" "Step aside from the crowd, ma'am." "What is in your pocket, ma'am?" Akilah hears the echoes in her head now, oozing out of the pavement's cracks. Her feet lose purchase. She does not want to hear the questions again, wants to go about without anybody assuming she's packing, wants to undulate her spine without anyone profiling her, charting her course. But the questions press in, surround her, arrow in.

⹑

The target is weaving, like drunk, like infected with the high spirits of the crowd, like poisoned by the SoMa vibe, a spirit high. He is wondering, comparing the picture one last time to this woman on the street. This is her, right? Akilah, cell organizer, protest queen, defiant woman pushing her chest high, her forehead open and lofty into the wind? No mistake.

⹑

Silent startle scream sticks in Akilah's throat. Where is she? When is she? Had she lost track of side streets, of the pavement's direction, of the place where she can step without encountering memories too hard to process, black skin splitting open on police batons, purple welts rising against rough brick walls? She goes down.

⹑

What happened? The assassin has lost sight of Akilah, hair bobbling down as passersby obscured his vision. He looks, hand shoves plastic stock back beneath his jacket, mustn't offer a tell to the street. Where is she?

&

The crack in the street, widening, moaning downward. Sadness pouring in dark tears, a wailing. Akilah falls into the street, beneath it, away from eyes and calls, from hails that forebode no well wishes. She falls, and she knows she does not need to scream. She gives. Cloth smooth, equatorial warmth, streaming reds and oranges. Akilah releases, opens, knees soften.

&

The proud black woman is gone. The federal assassin scans back and forth, has stopped the rental car at the side of the road. He looks back—no opening in the facades, just placid blank walls, no shops with open doors or invitations. Gone.

&

Akilah comes to, assembles, a calm over her. Twists wrist, clavicle shrug, knits pelvis to spine. She's lying on something rough, scaly. It is dark. There are glints in the darkness. They move. Is she moving? There is wind against her skin, in spurts: something seems to be pressing her along, in convulsive turns, but the something is too large for her to feel a direction. She is lying on a surface that shifts in space. That's all she knows for sure. To keep her fears beneath her, she presses her palms down, feels rills beneath her fingertips. She spreads her weight, in control.

The rills: these plates are not machined, not smooth poured metal. These are organic grown things, accreted. She scratches with one fingernail, like meeting like: is this horn? She is back at the image of a scale, articulating against others. She palpates. Akilah contemplates standing, but a sense of wind bursts dissuades her. She inches across the plate by turning on her front, on her hand and knees, pushing forward. Soon, she reaches the outer edges of the plate: a thick rind-like edge, horn, yes, layers and layers, as her hand reaches down. She lies on her belly and stretches. Her fingertips reach another surface, beneath, and yes, there is movement between that next plate and hers. Articulating scales or plates, indeed, in a counter motion, as if wrapped around moving limbs of some unseen giant beast. Akilah scrambles sideways, maps the contours of the plate. The shape feels ovular, but it's hard to be certain.

After a while, Akilah lies down on her back, face upward. She takes stock, retells what happens to cover over a blank in her mind: from the San Francisco street to this strange bed of darkness. She remembers the sidewalk, moving amid the theatre crowd, on her way to the protest action, the thinning of the sidewalk, even, now, in the back of her mind, the slow car advancing, a sense of dread that stumbled her feet. The sidewalk, opening like a door, a crack too regular for a normal earthquake, and her falling. She breathes, and senses behind her collarbone an answering breath: a beingness. A perceptual opening. Akilah is not sure what that means, exactly, but she takes it. She walks through.

"Hello."

"I am glad you are here."

"Where am I?"

"You are safe, for now. Safe from the gun. From the assassin. From the street."

"I belong on the street, though, with my sisters."

"You are a fighter. We know. We need you."

"Who are you?"

"We have been prophesized. We are here."

"What are you?"

"We are breathing beneath you. We hold you and see you. Receive this."

There is a pouring, a warmth, liquid, starting from a point inside her head. She accepts the water, diffuses it throughout her aching body. Fear trembles, then drowns.

She remembers when she had made that decision before, accepting the water. She had been six years old, and she had been visiting, her one visit outside the US. She had been flown all alone to Guyana, to grandmothers she cannot quite recall now, ancient hands with calluses caressing the spaces between her hair, a strange tickling. That day she had been playing outside near the jungle's edge, and there was a little stream, just so small, just the width of her young thigh, and she had knelt in it. And the water had swarmed over her, had climbed over her brown twig legs and arms. It had dripped off her head, spurted across her chest, glided down on her narrow back. And it had spoken, too, a faraway murmur she only now remembers again:

"We are here." Deep liquid inside her forehead, inside the precious round, a peach stone warming outward.

Akilah remembers telling one of her Guyanese grandmothers, in the home by the side of the road, on the porch nibbled by creepers.

"The little river spoke to me."

That's all she had said, and then she had fallen silent, and just stared at Nan's face, the mouth open, golden yellow teeth an intricate gate to a different world. A curled tongue hovered, trembling, in a pink gullet.

Akilah hadn't been scared then, not of the voice, not of her grandmother. She had been interested, had leaned into Nan's void, until the old woman had snapped shut her mouth, and had not spoken. Akilah knew then that the small hidden river had to be hers alone. The waters dripping so freely, so wide, was something that had to be kept apart, even from this elder love. And so she had shut it away, a turn of an iron key sealing the memory.

Now, here, on this scale, the key had shifted, had turned, and she bathed in the warmth of her six-year-old self, the flooding of sense and contraction new to her limbs, the ache of liquid love.

She wasn't hurt, and wouldn't be, not by government assassins, not by anybody. She was safe. But she was alone, and she missed her comrades. What world was this?

er

Tony shovels forkfuls of salad into his mouth. His left hand grips the edge of the table, hard, energy humming through, rattling the bolt that runs down into the floor's steel plating.

"Tony, relax."

Arina speaks quietly, but with insistence. He lowers the fork, consciously releases his death-grip on the steel tabletop. Opens his hand a few times, shooing away the cramp that threatens to descend. His ears are full with waves, with sounds like steel wool scratching: the planes thundering outside, beyond the plate glass window, the passers-by, thousands of feet drumming just feet away. Tony's heart beats alongside their pounding. He looks over his shoulder, till he feels Arina's cool hand on his arm.

"It's OK. She will be back soon."

He is not sure that he wants to hear the platitudes: his daughter has flown the coop, is off to school a few states away, and he had not even been allowed to drive her there, collapse her wheelchair for her, ready to pack. His daughter, who wants to take on the world, all the time, has to chain herself to inaccessible school buses, defy drivers who try to carry her up the bus stairs. His pepper baby.

He turns toward Arina's voice. There is her beloved mouth, still naturally pink against her wheat-white skin, small lines weaving across the fullness as if someone was making sure to focus hard, to paint each corner of this little face. He smiles at his wife of forty years.

Then he stares over Arina's shoulder at the concrete apron of the airport. Out there is Melanie's airplane, maybe waiting, last pre-flight checks, maybe already in flight, the old days of tracking the planes as they rumbled on their ballet long over. Out there.

Something is not right.

The concrete valley in front of his restaurant window heaves upward, a depression, then a boil, a breathing up and down. Halfway between their terminal and the opposite side, on the desert smoothness of light grey, something is being born. Up again—the yellow demarcation on the concrete shimmers in the afternoon sun as it undulates across the tarmac.

Arina turns, looks where Tony's staring.

She looks, first quiet, and then begins to scream when the first tentacles begin to shoot into the air.

Tony is up, shoving Arina in front of him as they shoo backwards from the window. He runs, dives into the main corridor of the terminal. Arina has not stopped screaming, and she is running out of air. He lifts her, a small weight compared to the heavy machinery of his body shop. They sprint toward the exit, out to the other side of the airport. He looks back, backs away from the nightmare, wet-looking fronds waving, tangles, growing out of slits in the concrete, weaving on the other side of the glass, exploring the airliner still peacefully waiting next to the bridge. Is this Melanie's airplane? The tentacles taste their way over the curved white skin of the plane.

The terminal doors still open, the electrics hadn't had enough time to shut down and lock down the airport. He rushes through, his heart pounding too loud in his ears. In the body shop the heavy machines get moved about by cranes now, and it has been a long time since he carried something as heavy as a body through the world. Arina glides from his suddenly limp arms.

"Tony. Sweetheart. Not now! Focus!"

With an immediate task at hand, Arina takes charge and hits Tony across his massive chest, startling his heart back into their predicament. Yes, he can walk. His girl might be in trouble, tentacled trouble beyond imagining. He turns and tries to sprint in bursts back into the terminal. A river of humans passes by. They see people drag carry-on suitcases along, nearly falling but reluctant to release their grip. One family is running from the terminal, blood dripping off the mother's face, a cut flowing freely. Many have dumped their bags, and run with the abandon of unfettered limbs. Others, seeing their example, seeing the blood, drop their bags, too, and start to sprint away. The bags remain, though, and create a new obstacle course, spin with their old momentum only half spent. One large purple bag rolls down the slope under its own steam, trundling across the intersection, and folds into a thin white woman, knifes her legs out from under her. Tony sees it, and sees it for what it is: the beginning of a deadly panic. Some of these people will be trampled, long before any monster can reach them.

Arina wails, claws at him, tries to reverse their direction and leave this space. He pulls them both out of the main flow, back toward the windows, tries to quickly explain what he saw, the tentacles tapping their way over the airliner.

"Arina. Wait. We need to check on Melanie. What if she's still in the plane out there?"

They turn together. Look out of the huge bay windows, out at the airport. Beyond the terminal, on the tarmac, it happens. It blooms. The tip of the airliner is sucked in, then out, shooting outward on a firestorm. The plane is an inferno, its flames a heat wave rushing outward. Tony sees the tentacles in the airfield loop then whoosh down, vanish. Time expands, then the deep boom of the explosion travels over Arina and Tony and all the other fleeing people.

Melanie isn't on the disintegrated plane, bombed to bits. She isn't on the tarmac, either, burning up in kerosene flames. Melanie isn't quite sure where she is, at this point. She saw the tentacles emerge on the runway, saw a rubber-like tip entwine the titanium spokes of her wheelchair, carefully, lifting her high up, and then down, through the earth, just as a boom above sent a heat wave down after her.

She is in darkness. A deep vibrating sound pulses through her bones. She is lying against a giving wall, not cold exactly, but cooler than flesh, warmer than earth. Smooth, with ridges that press into her own contours. She can't quite get the sequence right. Mum and Dad had driven her to the airport, sure, had hugged her goodbye, and she had wheeled through security. She had been ready to enter the airplane, had been about to transfer from her wheelchair onto the aisle chair to be loaded. And then...

She just can't quite recall, although there is a ripping sound in her head, a sound sheet metal might make if sheared apart, a spatial sound, like something shifting direction as the metal curves downward. Then the tentacle, grey and pink, and so careful and caring. Are her parents alright? What happened to everybody? Now there is ... thickness and rubber. That's what the surface feels like, like the inside of a car tire, not the smoothness of the inner tube, but the rough substantial feel she remembers from crawling around her dad's wrecking yard, playing hide-and-seek in the tire pile.

Her hand explores. Tire, tire, tire, rubber welt, another— then a slit. Her hand goes in, sideways, deep. She immediately takes it out again, not sure what her left pinkie fingertip had felt deep in there: slime? Water? She pulls the hand closer, in the darkness, and smells the side: no odor, really, just a whiff of airport soap and, just beneath it, something a bit mold-like, dank. Huh.

Melanie remembers old cellar rooms, Michigan basements, with that smell deep in the corners where the spiders live. She had enjoyed visiting with the spiders, bumping down the steep stairs on her butt. As a tiny one, she had delighted in the feel of small legs on her limbs, the frantic spider climbing a smooth, white, rolling mountain.

Laying her hands again against the rubber she concentrates on her feet. She can feel them much more than usual. Secure, on a small ledge or ring, circular, raised against the equally circular wall she's leaning on. She tests the ring, and it holds as she drops her weight harder, bounces up a little, as much as her weak knees allow. No problem there.

And then there is. The curved surface in front of her shifts in the darkness, and gravity becomes a player. And tips her. Her weak feet lose the ring ground, and grope, scrabble, as the ring lifts backward, away from her. Her hands hold on for a second more, tension between them creating an adhesion, but not for long. Melanie falls, but everything feels too close, too dark, to really panic. She stretches out both arms as she tips backward, spread-eagled in descent, eyes open. No light falls in.

Falling. Is this a second yet? She is curiously comfortable. Melanie is not counting, is spinning silk in her mind, ropes to hurl and sail on. Concentrate.

Abruptly, she stops falling. Without much sensation, she is pressed against a second hard surface, this time against her back. Her hands feel out and again the feel is hard, hard like old rubber, like rubber past oil and street grit and water hosing and maybe even a fire hard. There are ridges, again, these ones uneven, older, as if more exposed to the elements than the earlier surface.

There was no impact, and she does not hurt. She can hear that she is no longer alone. Which feels good.

"Hello?"

Melanie asks of the scrabbling off to her side, a human

touching noise, not an insect pattern.

"Hello." The answering voice is deeper than her own, but a woman, too. Alto. Calm.

"I just arrived. Where am I?" Melanie ventures.

"I do not know. I arrived here a short while ago, from a pavement in San Francisco."

"Really? I was at Denver Airport, just getting onto a plane. I had just left my parents. I need to make sure they are OK. But where are we?"

"Can you remember what happened?"

"No, not really. Just a sound. An opening. A tentacle lifting me up. Then falling downward, but soft."

"Yes. That's me, too. No sound, just a sensation of going down in the street. Like something opening. No tentacle, but yes, some kind of creature. Big. And now I am here, and there are voices."

"Voices?"

As Melanie reaches out with her mind, full of curiosity, she hears them, too: voices around her, beneath her waist, echoing in her lungs, trembling along her femur. She sits up, much easier than she had ever done in her wheelchair, and listens inside.

"Welcome."

Melanie hears the voice, recognizes its cadence, as if all terror and uncertainty rush out into the world in one word, then transform. She faints.

er

Akilah hears the tumble in the blackness of the scale night, and rushes forward. Melanie folds into her arms. They sit, one draped over the other, on the scale moving in the night. Akilah fears nothing, knows no pain, as she sings to and is sung to by the voices, waiting for Melanie to come back. She is a young one. She is glad to have a comrade again. A girl, twisted lower body and legs, but breathing.

Melanie's eyelashes flutter against Akilah's neck, her breath changes rhythm. Now she is back.

"What surprised you?" A warm mouth whispers in her ear.

"I know that voice. It's been a long time, I had forgotten." Melanie whispers back, keeping close to the warm human skin and blood that is holding her now.

"Tell me."

"It's the spider voice. In the cellar. Spun me in softest silk, right across my eyes, one night...." Melanie's voice recedes a bit, in memory, soft like a warm river in Akilah's ear, open and vulnerable.

"I heard it too, before, in a small river far away. It's good."

"It's good. It has come back before." Melanie remembers nights that had terrified her co-protestors, lying on cold pavements in schoolbus yards, limbs twisted over chains they had padlocked shut. Campaigning for ramps and access points, against nursing homes and locking people away. Bringing it all out into the open. They had thrown the keys away, long parabolas of tiny silver twinkles into the far bushes. She had heard the spider voice then, rolling, holding, spinning cocoons. She had heard the spider voice when they broke into a juvenile care facility, lifted each other over broken windows, to visit with incarcerated youths, their alter egos, holding each other on slim cots. The voice had draped silks over her and her cot mate, a round brown teenager, hair shaved, softest down, eyelashes trembling. The voice had whispered to them. The youths they visited had been frightened, elated, and then exhausted, adrenaline mixing with the juices of lying close, of sensual touch. Melanie shakes away this memory, uncurls from Akilah's lap just a bit, to open a space for talk.

"What are we doing here? Where are we? Who are you?"

They shift apart, introduce themselves.

Melanie. New student, disability activist, access specialist.

On her way to head out to Pitzer College, Southern California.

Akilah. Poet, dancer, on her way from a Black Lives Matter protest in San Francisco.

They are flying, alive, into the night, together, into their futures. This scale is too small to hold them, and it is not their place to stay here, they both know that. They are needed elsewhere. But it is clear the world is shifting, something is being born. What does it want of them? Melanie thinks of her parents, misses them. But that is not the way forward.

Melanie takes Akilah's hand. She is ready to respond to the voice. Akilah is ready, too. She grasps Melanie's hand, transmits her resolve. They get up. Melanie teeters on her weak legs, leans against Akilah, feels her own side melting into Akilah's hip. In that other woman's hip, she can feel echoes of water, rivers, of green against street grey. Melanie is full of resolve, of spider warmth, metal spokes, and tensile strength. Akilah feels the smoothness, clarity, in Melanie's warm palm.

The darkness around them is full and warm, an entity pressing against their eyes. The voices come.

"Help us rebuild."

"Where are my parents? Are they OK?"

"We do not know."

Akilah hurts knowing there is no one person who claims her heart right now. Her grandmothers are dead, her parents, long settled far away. Her comrades, in fight.

"We do not know, but we need you. They need you, too, after the bombs and the fires. We need to build. Are you ready?"

Together, they step to the edge of the scale. They step off.

VICKI'S CUP

Vicki is in the back of Vicki's Cup, her coffee store, carefully pouring thick chilled milk into the fragrant mixture. Cinnamon and a hint of chili float in the air and tickle the inside of her nose. Ahead of her, her employees Carlos and Lucy are arranging plump chocolate bonbons into small boxes, ready to go out to the snake of students winding into the street. Everywhere are open white faces, one brown face here or there, all out for their daily shot of rich dark mocha to help their day along.

Her iced spiced Mexican mocha drink has become legendary since she opened her little store four short years ago. Vicki gives thanks each night at the small altar, still well hidden by a last divider, invisible to the public in the front of the store. Her solid, anchored store. Thanks for finding this perfectly suited place of old traffic and exchange; thanks for sending her here, to these particular woods of learning; thanks for getting her out of a suburban Dodge City half-forgotten and never missed. May it never change.

She smiles, and starts to prepare a new batch. Turned away from the counter, Vicki raises her hand and strokes her forefinger with a small golden comb, an aquamarine jewel set in a tight claw at its end. An infinitesimal shiver of skin cells sloughs off under the golden urging, and sails into the mixer.

et

Carlos observes Vicki, his eyes turned all the way to the left, turned so hard his muscles are hurting, straining behind his long, luxurious lashes. Vicki's round form effectively keeps him from whatever is going on with her hands. For weeks now, he's been trying to work out her secret.

He's even tried once to make his own batch, combining the luscious ingredients that line the sides of the store with the best coffee beans he could find—for Vicki's own coffee beans are securely locked away each night. The result was delicious, certainly, but not quite right. "Not quite right," that had been the verdict of coffee stores for miles around, all of them desperate to work out the secret of Vicki's chocolatier empire, a secret she keeps in her velvet-swathed bosom, behind a small golden crucifix.

Carlos's dream is to manage a little chain paradise, underlings and customers, coffee smells and creamy liquids his daily bread. What are a few months' worth of snooping against this dream? All that stands between him and the desired title is Vicki's recipe. If he can get it, hasta la vista barista, hi there, store manager.

"Celibacy? You mean, no sex?" Carlos had been quite perplexed by this unusual request put down, quite matter of fact, during his interview.

"No sex. Kissing is ok. But no genital contact with anybody, same sex or other."

"It's a Catholic store?" Carlos had enough semi-nuns in his family, and enough sparkly saint images around his old homestead. For a second, during that first interview, he wavered, wondered about his dream of ventis, aromas and shots, and how far he had really travelled.

"No. Not Catholic. You can love whoever you like, worship whoever you like. But on the evenings before the days you work here, no sex. It's an energy thing. Other nights, whatever."

"Huh. Ok." It's not like Carlos got it that regularly. And how would Vicki know, anyway? But somewhere deep inside, a little Carlos worm turned. She would know. He knew. But he wanted this, wanted the secret, wanted the warm wood paneling of his own store, wanted the keys to the bathroom, wanted his own stack of New York Times papers crisp and inviting, wanted a kingdom of coffee amid the snow.

"Ok. I can do it."

That had been two months ago. Since then, no progress. He still does not know what makes the mocha so special. And his own little empire is still waiting.

&

Lucy can't figure it out. Carlos is all distracted again, checking out Vicki. Vicki! Twice his age, at least. What is it with the damn mocha. Crying into mixing pots, most likely, and that's how Vicki grabs the Carlos Casanovas and the college queens.

Lucy tries to lean forward, her top button still open in what feels like sinful abandon to her. She's ready to scream, but she knows this won't help. Instead, she sighs deeply, and enjoys the tug of the rough cotton blouse across her bra. Her floury hands find her dark curls, pat them into place here and there.

Oh damn. She's done it again. A quick look in a small mirror mounted on the wall shows hair covered in white flour dust, and a big smear on her glasses, too.

"Bathroom break, ok?" Carlos barely nods, his attention still elsewhere.

Lucy tries to undo the damage to her hairdo, and polishes her glasses till they shine. She sighs and fingers the small leather sack that dangles between her breasts. Is this helping her at all? She isn't sure, and might have to step up the program a bit.

For now, she fishes her eyeliner out of the small cosmetic bag hidden behind the toilet paper rolls, and begins the long procedure of painting deep dark wings above her green eyes. She stares into the mirror, her eyes wide, unblinking, and lets her hands linger on the roughness of her blouse, fingering seams and contours, till her breath quickens and she can see the rose in her cheeks.

74

*e*r

Vicki notices the heavy weaponry immediately upon Lucy's return. She smiles to herself. The hormonal waves of her employees work for her—as long as they do not consummate their passions on worknights, that is. And there is no resolution in sight: Lucy can pine as much as she likes, Carlos is hardly likely to go down this path, his eyes set on less soggy prey.

She feels compassion for Lucy, her late twenties putting her on a shelf in this college town more firmly than Victorian mores might have done. Lucy might have better luck in one of the bigger cities that ring this spot of forested idyll. But Vicki knows that Lucy, like so many, isn't likely to leave soon. The memories of college aren't easily dimmed by poverty-line jobs and no benefits, and by the sense of excitement that each September brings along. This is home to the Lucys of this world, a chance of redemption each year, a new set of deadlines for writers who peck away at their nascent novels each November, with a brew of Colombian coffee thick and bubbly at their side.

Lucy once showed Vicki one of her stories, on an afternoon when business was slow. A thick wad of paper print-outs, sprawled over with black ink, whole lines illegible beneath the second-guessing pen, additions in spidery hand-writing, the 'g's rounded with a slight lean to the right, drunken matrons propping up against the unrelenting print lines.

Vicki let Lucy read a page or so. She could hear the sadness dripping out, scenes of remembered child abuse and longing for strangers, met for an hour at a time on railway journeys across the nation, Amtrak journeys that ended years ago, when Lucy lost her student health insurance and gained more work hours in jobs that allowed for the slow dreaminess of a writer's haze, for the emotional thickening of unmet desires. She gave Lucy a special mocha, extra large, and let her hand smooth down one of Lucy's wayward locks, caught akimbo across the top of her forehead.

Vicki turns back to her cauldron, and stirs. The heady aromas of pheromones, tinged with darker scents, delight her senses, and she feels her own blood up and roiling.

er

Punctually at six, Vicki closes shop. Carlos tries to linger a bit, but Vicki knows her secret is too well guarded to be in danger. Carlos's world does not include her own realities, and because of that he'll never find out. Lucy, on the other hand, is more aware of wider vibrations, but any lingering she engages in has more to do with what fills Carlos's pants than with the content of Vicki's pots. Vicki shoos them out. Her employees disappear down the street, Carlos quickly pushing past Lucy, her more leisurely pace faltering even further upon being overtaken. Ah well. Puppy love. Vicki wishes, not for the first time, that Lucy were a better candidate for a life of devotion to a different flesh. There had been some promise. She could have helped her. But as it is, Vicki can offer Lucy a paycheck, and that is not bad, either. Vicki pulls down the blind, and the store and workshop fall dark.

er

Not too far away, a car is hurtling toward the delicious chocolate pots of Vicki's Cup. Margot drives through the dusk, her hands loosely on the wheel, her mind working herself through other mileposts. The car is new, speedy, a lovely present from her husband, but Margot can't find enough pleasures in its sleek lines. Ten years out from her doctorate, she is still adjuncting her way up and down South Michigan and Ohio, two hours in a futuristic glass and steel sculpture, three hours in a utilitarian box, fifty minutes at yet another small college with well-tended ivy and with no intention of hiring her full-time. Ten years of tired slog, punctuated by dozens of applications that go nowhere, and by brief snatches of time too short to do research and write, only enough time to mourn the loss of that precious time.

Her students. The thank-yous from the really eager ones, the ones that do want to go on, the ones that are sparked by Margot's own passion for Victorian women writers: women these students have never heard of, but who become objects of fantasy and veneration in hours spent in dusty library rooms, passports out and into other worlds of crinolines and bombazine scratching against heated skin. The shrugs of the ones who have their minds elsewhere, who sit in her classroom because they have to. The many in between. Margot loves the classroom, loves to nourish these lovely malleable brains in front of her, sees past their deer-like long limbs and the soft down that covers bare thighs. But Margot's clock is running out, has run out, and there is no way to turn it back.

Margot can't see herself in an office job, nine-to-five, pumps and hose. Oh no, that's not the life she had ever imagined, sitting quietly in her father's study, watching him bowed over his anthropology texts, bowing her own head in imitative turn. She does not want to fill out forms and design surveys, or fiddle with marketing copy.

So here she is. Her silky shirt, brushing against her bare breasts. She shifts and feels the fabric against her nipples. Her still tight bottom fills out her best jeans, and she swishes in her car seat, knowing her assets. Ready to feed young minds, to cleave to the flame of Education. She imagines herself a Phoenix, ready to fly through the fire, and sees feathers tinged in red and orange, bursting into flames, as she follows the taillights of another car down the turnpike.

She also pictures herself as a martyr, glowing iron and red oozing sores, remembers hagiography texts, stories of the saints and their suffering. The University, for a shining moment, becomes a toga-clad woman, a loving caressing goddess, mother and lover, ready to hold her sad child to her breast. Margot longs to be held, to nuzzle, to lick.

Margot knows these visions for the self-indulgent bullshit they are, old-time projections of tenured bliss that have little relation to education business today, years of frustration channeled into images that arise out of old books. She knows, but so what. The life she wants is out of reach, will never be hers, and it isn't entirely clear to her if it's anybody's life anymore, anyway. But no matter. She has had enough. No more telling her lawyer brother about new publications in her field, dulcet ramblings and sweet exclamations, as if she really cares. As if she really has time to read all the crap that flows over the Modern Language Association's tables. She's pretty certain her brother has seen through this, long ago.

One way or another, this solution will mean the end of summer barbeques of sadness. Which is the point, right? She adjusts the air conditioning in the car, and sits straighter, focused.

et

One hour and a few small preparatory procedures later, a tentative knock sounds on the back door of Vicki's Cup. Vicki opens. Her date this evening comes from one of the great urban areas to the East. The woman enters, curiously, a bit nervous, but with the straight back of finality. Vicki can smell the new car odor on her. Vicki's eyes soften when she takes in her guest's sweet form, the Guatemalan velvet scarf over new jeans, the carefully prepared loose hair, and the pink bud of a mouth, eternally dewy and fresh with the wonders of lip glaze. Vicki breathes in deeply, watches her date's eyes follow the swell of Vicki's bosom, the breath steadying them both.

"Come in, my dear. No talking, please, let us be silent for a while," Vicki says quietly, with authority, but warm. She takes her guest's light summer jacket, and folds it neatly, depositing it on a dresser by the door, not to be forgotten.

"Ok, no talking. That's good. Yes." A whispered reply. She can see her date relieved, relaxing.

Vicki reaches up, and the woman steps into the beginning of an embrace. Brown fingers caress red hair, fingers trail over moisturized, only slightly lined skin. The other woman sighs, already responding with a slight give in her knee joints, her shoulders descending. Vicki feels her own power rising, her feet firmly planted in the exact middle of the chocolate shop's gleaming woods, her celebrant's role exultantly clear. At the high point of her teachings, her mentors' hands on her back, on her round dimpled buttocks, Vicki grasps the other woman's head, an excited tremor in her careful fingers. She bows the woman's face down to her own upturned lips, four eyes slowly closing. Their mouths meet, eager, now hungry. Vicki offers the pill of chocolate fat on her own tongue, lets Margot's tongue work in her own mouth. Throughout, Vicki listens to Margot's fingertips on her skin, feels the nuance of trace and exploration, until she is ready to judge.

et

Rose-colored light breaks through the gaps around the window coverings. The light hits a few dust motes, remnants of old skins and time, drifting in the shop's currents. Beneath the swirling air the floor planks of the old store gleam in rich grained red. Vicki is on her knees, yet another bucket of dirty water beside her, scrubbing back and forth. Her back moves in the rhythms of ritual, polishing, erasing, spreading, soaking.

Water spreads over the old wood, tracing old trails of tree life, knots and grain patterns. No consummated adolescent groping, no dripping semen's release spoils the immaculate

79

stream. Passion, pure and simple. In water, air and wood, hormones mingle and release a botanical steam that carries a hint of rain forests and faraway lands.

The traffics of the world have always nourished the university and its explorers, and the patterns haven't changed. Willingly they come, in ecstasy, and lay their contact hours on the altar's salver. Their sacrifice keeps the machines of knowledge oiled. After a lifetime spent in dusty libraries they receive their new passports here, flights to Paraguay or Ecuador pre-arranged, new identities to vanish into the South. They gain entry into a life of sweat and sun, collecting the cherries and watching the green turn brown. Unlined academic hands with tender fingertips pick each coffee cherry when it is just ripe, eyes and minds accustomed to look for minute changes are now keeping watch over the patterns of little trees in the mountains. In the calm and quiet of the hut, Margot will join her brethren and lay out the harvested fruit in the sun, turn them and nurse them in their month-long drying. The few electric outlets in the long narrow sleeping hut host kindle chargers, and there's wifi to connect to the digitalized ancient book collections the world over. Vicki licks her lips, tastes again Margot's sweet kiss. She'll do fine. Deep passion, in abeyance, well used to the delay of gratification, and the tenderness of things. She'll stroke the beans carefully, gently, her touch just right. Perfect. That's the one secret Carlos will never know. That's the non-reciprocal tenderness that eludes Lucy.

Vicki thinks about the hacienda, and allows herself a moment of longing for sunshine and the fragrant note of the drying shed. And for the soft, soft hands of the ones that are ready to let go and enter new service, the ones she has sent South, to the lands she has longed to visit herself for so long. She will have to arrange her holiday flights.

Spice and sweetness float in the air, and behind Vicki, the large pots stand ready.

er

Margot wakes up with her nose deep in fragrant leaves, as she has every day for these last two years. Her mattress is strewn with the vibrant green leaves, now curling in as they dry. Soon, she will replace them. The day stretches ahead. It's off season—early days into the nine months in which the coffee does not present itself for harvest. She is laid off, but nowhere as badly off as her comrades in the surrounding plantations. Like many of her fellows here at La Casa Libra, she reads, their minuscule savings from the old life still tiding them over here, where a US dollar looks like a gold coin. Margot listens for her neighbors, many of them awakening, stumbling to the outdoor restroom, or, like her, quietly reading their way into the day, before the first precious cup of delicious black gold.

Today, though, she's getting bored. She hadn't really counted on this, the endless repetition of readings, working, surfing the web, maybe teaching a class or two of English to the village kids. Going for a walk. Stretching her brown limbs, strong and supple, maybe going for a swim. It's fine. But it's boring, the way a new car glides from scent delight to necessity in daily handling. She closes her eyes again, and tastes once more Vicki's chocolate offering, the feel of a living tongue on hers. She tries to remember her husband's morning caresses, but breaks off when that does little to arouse her. She could find sex here easily, if she wanted it, but that's not quite the challenge she's seeking.

Margot has analyzed the market situation, made herself familiar with the economics of coffee growing, the seasons, the laborers, and what the world-wide patterns of consumptions do to local economies of coffee growers. She has read widely, blogs and books, connected with the finest university libraries on her laptop. And she still speaks with the kids, the eager ones and the bored ones, finds out about their world, their parents, their siblings, and the plantations.

She tracks a beetle making its way over her coverlet, its eight black piston legs tasting and touching its way to the seam's edge. It shifts direction, stops for a while to pick up the precious skin debris that she has left in her bedding. She should squash the beetle, kick it to the curb before it devours the secret ingredient. That's what she was asked to do. By now, Margot has found out everything about the secret spice, the essence distilled from her own pure, dedicated life, a life of showering in coffee tea leaf, sleeping in its heady embrace, eating chocolates and syrups to prepare and live her devout life. But recently, it has become harder to guard the world's intellect juice, and to keep the borders tight, the rules in sight. The beetle continues on its journey, small sounds clicking their way to Margot's ears. She bows nearer, reverently, and sees herself reflected in the greens and blues that shimmer in the beetle's carapace. But something licks up inside her, a beetle flame, a new idea.

et

Vicki stands between her coffee pots. It's still her all alone here, in the mornings, every morning, before the big crew of assistants comes in. Carlos is long gone, of course, and now heads a specialty tea shop in a small town a few valleys over, full of tea of the month gimmicks, mail orders and changing menus. Lucy is still around, half-time now that her novel has finally sold. She's still soppy and scarlet lipped, but no longer in so much need.

Vicki has her tablet in her hand, her feet frozen to the cool winter tiles. She stares at the dreadful message sent by her old teachers. The supply chain is broken. She reads about a pirate queen, a rebel, a swashbuckling woman with red hair, carrying off a whole year's worth of drying pods and secret sachets in the middle of the night. Vicki's eyes drift to the pots, to the bubbles that form in her last batch of mocha. In the steam that rises, she can see a sailing ship, a slope in full sail, heading out to the foggy seas.

II: Crystals

THE WHEELCHAIR RAMP

Joshi wheeled over rough wood. She reached down, felt the residual warmth of early fall in the grain. She pulled herself further along by grasping the metal railing. Ice cold sweet on her fingers. She pushed, and her wheels glided upward. She was on a wide ramp, an art project erected in this condemned block of wooden homes and churches, a Latino neighborhood of Grand Rapids. Her wheelchair reached the ramp's apex and its flow changed, a freewheeling moment of suspension unaided by her fingers. She laughed, roared along the open platform, wind in her black hair.

She climbed a last segment and centered herself in the middle of the keep, snug and upright in her wheelchair's seat, sides clasped by bright plastic. This last bit of the ramp led nowhere. It was suspended over empty ground, creeping alongside the old wooden building but extending beyond it. From here, she could look through the ramp's metal railing to survey the land around her: empty buildings, shaped by age, now reshaped by installation artists. This was a fortuitous site to meet her blind date. Derelict elements artfully stripped and patched, now combined into rhythmic patterns of hope. Anything could happen here. New sensations could reach out of gaps and fissures. She checked her bright red watch. One minute to go.

Joshi looked away from the gently ticking watch. She checked the alignment of her booties on the footrest. Adjusted her scarf, fluffed her thick hair. Tugged the leather jacket tight around her torso. She looked sharp, she knew, sartorially savvy graduate student playing with the archetypes of power and sex. No oriental kitten here in red roar lipstick.

A number of people had stepped onto the platform just beneath her, along the first long incline. Would her date be among them? She saw two middle-aged women, sandaled, sweaters.

No way. One lonely man with a camera, arranging shots of the crisscrossing wood and metal, crouching and skipping. Unlikely. A family: man, woman, two blonde kids tiredly drooping in their parents' clutch. And there she was. Yes. She was bound to be her blind date, yes please.

A large woman, white like so many of the visitors here around art-city, but marked with tribal signs Joshi could decode: a large tattoo in her neckline, single color red linen top under bright fleece jacket. Black leggings with pleather inserts. Voluptuous lines.

Joshi's hands twitched just looking. She waved. The woman waved back, not fazed at all, no double take visible. Joshi had identified herself as a wheelchair-user and a grad student, had given that much at least, before putting her lot into the electronic hat of the blind date lottery. She had no need to see pity blossom in anybody's eyes, old stories that were not hers draped around her by foreign minds. This woman looked like she could deal. Joshi let out a deep breath she didn't know she'd been holding.

The woman's boots clomped up the ramp to the aerie. Joshi felt the rhythm of the woman's legs in her seat, the ship-like motion of the wood's give, translated into sensitive sit bones. She watched the vision in red and black climb to her, leaning into the grade.

et

And there Joshi was, her hands reaching out from the house that the twister ate, in Oklahoma, so many summers ago. That day she had been the girl cut by the edge, left alone and crying. Her parents, who had made their trek to Vietnamese orphan homes, and who had held out their sweet lined hands, now lay crushed beneath metal spikes and rafters. Joshi's teenage hands climbed and climbed, spiders concentrating on scratching, sound-making, forward motion. That night Joshi had lost her legs to metal and wood, to the crunch of ceilings coming down like pistons. She had lost feet, calves, knees, thighs. Had lost ghosts of her white family. Had gained hardware: rubber, screws, new knobs and gears.

The spider child had crawled, mewled, protested and rallied, till the ceiling burst open when the rescue crew found her. She had reached, and hands had come down past lathe and plaster, had grasped, pulled, and blankets, fluids, time, time, more time. White time. Red time. Hospital time.

Her favorite nurse, LeighAnn, warm voice and mother song, telling her stories of smoking weed on the back of corvettes at Wayne State tailgate parties, of going out with football stars, stories of nightblack yards and velvet skin.

et

On the ramp, Joshi blinked, focused on the wetness of rusty water on her hand, the drizzle on her neck, like her therapist had taught her. Come back, girl. Shh, girl. Here, girl.

She twisted her wheels against one another, a ballet in place, a racehorse nibbling at the stable door. The woman, her blind date, was coming nearer, and Joshi liked the dark hair, the dark eyes, the carefully shaped eyebrows. The bosom firm, encased, the bow of a boat under the red fabric, parting the mists. Joshi smiled now, made sure to keep herself open and in the now. But then, for one second, she looked beyond the approaching woman, and her eyes climbed up the exposed sinews of the condemned house skeletons around her, climbed their lathe layers one by one, a mathematics of escape.

et

The twister had held the house for a short time in its eye, in its spiral coil. Joshi saw the tentacle of bricks and wood hovering above her, every single one heavy enough to crush her, to end her probing gaze. The bricks had spun on in their complex dance, energies rushing out and up. The tornado's snout had sucked in chairs and wardrobes, splintering wood into eye-piercing shards. The circle hole in the sky had sucked, and sucked, and she had been horizontal for a while, her hands entwined in the pipes of the kitchen sink, till the eyes closed, and the column collapsed over her pelvis.

et

Her blind date. She had shifted space, was now here, like the girl in *Ringu*, jump cut.
"Hello. Joshi?"
A melodious voice asked, reminding her of LeighAnn, of painkillers, of laughter, of boys, of cars on wet fall nights at the drive-in. Joshi nodded, her larynx dry and closed tightly shut. The woman opposite her seemed to know.
"I am Lorna. Nice to meet you. What a great place for a date!"
Joshi had nodded, eyes pleading, wide, her hands fluttering like hummingbirds at her side. Her voice was gone, gone, time split.

et

Lorna shimmered deep inside herself, felt her fascia unclasping. Long sheets of fiber reached into her muscles, membranes connected sectors of pulsing tissue. She was walking, stopping, standing. Her feet heaved up, down, in a rhythm that was distinctly her own, slight hitch here, the self-consciousness of successful physical therapy.

The slight incline of the ramp had put extra pressure on her calves, as her figure bent into the lean. She felt the blood pulsing there, too. Every step massaged her muscles from inside. Blood beat. Lymph moved. Her juices, coursing. She let her fingers trail along the rough railing. Cool steel. The tiny dimples of beginning rust offered texture.

Every sensation was intense, new, still full of the excitement of reconnecting nerves. Before she lost herself in her body's spectacular alignment, though, she looked up, at the young woman in the intricate wheelchair, perched high up on the top ledge of the ramp. Lorna liked the wheelchair's clean geometry, its metal lines and steel origami. She also liked what she saw of the young woman: dark leather, tight posture, fingers on the wheel's rim. A black mane cascading over the black leather.

A motorcycle fantasy flitted over Lorna's memory screen. She had always liked the fast ones, wheels and dust.

She took the next step, upward. The wood under her feet showed the memory of trees, the branch holes and contours of age rings. The tree had grown for a long time, before being hewn down and planed into wide sheets.

Lorna flashed back to her own wood memory, to the moment when her blood stained and watered moon canals, whorls of ancient grain preserved in man-made stone. It had been concrete that crushed her. Concrete pressed between wooden plates, imprinted with the growths and patterns of a tree's fingerprint.

In the blink of an eye, Lorna was back between the pancaked layers of a grey, bare New Zealand corridor. It had happened on her way to the swimming pool in Christchurch. The smell of chlorine in her nose. The moist warmth of the heated rooms heavy, condensing on her glasses. She had walked through a modernist ode to progress and efficiency, grey, flat, raw material brutal and real all around her. She couldn't wait to escape into the weightlessness of the water.

Then it had happened, quick and slow at the same time, in a dizzying heave. The corridor wall had shifted toward her, jump cut, both left and right, converging on her. The wood-patterned concrete had come nearer, ever nearer, to the polyester of her swimming suit, to her painted toes, to her outstretched hands, closing in with every heave and tremor of the earth. Smaller chunks had arrived first, had pressed first cool and moist, then harder, into her limbs. Their sharp edges had ground their own imprints into her yielding flesh. Eventually, her skin had split.

Lorna rarely had flashbacks and this wasn't quite one, either. There was no panic, no sense of doom or hopelessness. She walked on the ramp, anchored. She had escaped that pool hallway, had been pulled from the earthquake rubble, after many hours staring at the ever encroaching cold grey fake concrete wood. Fake. Concrete. Wood.

That had been a long time ago. It was past. But here were the patterns anew beneath her feet, real wood, for certain, in its own raw authenticity. There was this kinesthetic, inward feeling of disorientation, the slight pull of unusual pressure on the backs of her legs. She tried to think about new lovers, not about old blood in chlorine water. Lorna was ok. She was ok.

No. She wasn't. No. But she had tools. She breathed. Stopped the ascent. Assembled her tools. There, in a clock's tick, as she wasn't ok, she fled to the warmth of the therapy pool, on her back, no weight on or in her, floating, floating. Open. Breathe. Feel the water.

The soft rain on her face helped. It cooled her. Lorna was fine, just fine. She stepped forward again, the moment of hesitation gone, conquered.

Ahead was Joshi. Ahead was a new person to explore. Joshi's wheelchair fascinated Lorna, and she longed to explore its contours with her hands, on someone else's body, a body molded by fissures and angles of metal and plastic. She longed to feel the plastic seat radiating a flesh bottom's heat.

That's why she had entered the date lottery—to meet a wheelchair-using woman, to see how life could go on, how wholeness could take on new meanings. She had earned her strange desires. And she would confess, eventually, once the fantasy liaison became more than a fetish meeting, if and when this young woman reached deeper inside her. Eventually.

Her fingers were again on the railing. They followed her momentum, took direction from steel's flowing melt. Upward.

"I love installation art."

Lorna did, she really did. She was happy to say it out loud. She wanted to make this beautiful creature in front of her understand. Lorna loved installations, their offerings to her body. She travelled far and wide to see the kind of installations that offered a new home to a body chopped up, mediated, transformed. Lorna wanted to inhabit. To find the angular walls of home. To run from the walls. To touch and lick and squish herself close.

She spoke again, as the young woman in front of her was silent, but attentive.

"I love it. I am so glad you chose this site. Thank you."

et

Joshi still couldn't speak, but her face was open, upward, glowing. The woman called Lorna seemed to see her.

The woman called Lorna knelt down, right there, on the wet wood of the ramp, out over the street. She knelt, and it was as if a wave of red and black rolled over the ramp, surrounded Joshi, warm and close, disorienting.

"It's ok. I am an architect. I am a surgeon. I am a poet. I am a dreamer."

Had she really said that? Had she? Joshi blinked, saliva flowing gently, slowly, a new river deep inside. In front of her, Lorna blinked, gently, held herself at bay, hovering. A dream woman. Was she here? She had dark eyes, lashes like iron posts, an offering of sanctuary. Joshi tried to speak, couldn't, felt for her parents' love, couldn't, thought of the maze of masonry and kitchen pipes, and the dancing, dancing bricks.

In front of her, Lorna's hands sunk into the wood of the ramp. Joshi saw Lorna's fingernails lengthen, grow lines and whorls. Hands folded right into the wood grain. Now she knew what to do, how to respond to the invitation. Joshi pulled forward, her wheelchair wheels, sensitive and light, curling into Lorna's palm. They fit as if into grooves. Joshi felt her pelvis widen, sink, a metal filigree that began to unclasp from the bottom of her wheelchair seat. The pelvis metals drilled down, wings and cantilevers, angles. Lorna's head reached up, her throat's tender underside open and warm. Joshi leaned in, her lips finding the warm rosy skin ahead of her. Lorna's head slowly came down, her dark hair cascading into dark dogwood twigs. Their mouths met. Copper. A tiny clash of enamel.

Metal and wood, they shifted into their puzzle form, clicking into place. They molded, like a ship's plank bowed over steam. Curve and angular containment. The rain started and the ramp's planks steamed into mist.

THE NURSING HOME

"Just like a puzzle box," the old storyteller said, his hands accompanying this often-repeated tale with small intricate gestures, "we saw it curving and folding in on itself. Such a noise. In the end, it slid right off the cliff, down into the sea. All were lost."

Three soaked campers experienced the story come to its peak, yet again, and shifted in their bamboo or merino clothes to keep the evening chill at bay. The rock they hovered on felt newer with each glimpse of nature's destruction, boiling columns of smoke and wet tumbling rock, the end of the Shoreside nursing home.

They had made camp on bare rock, somewhat flat, slightly hollow, a welcome secure perch after scrambling up through too many bramble patches and miles of squishy mud. Jonathan was the first to split away after another story of Shoreside's day of disaster. He headed out to the edge of the rock plane, and wordlessly began to strip off his damp outerwear before inserting himself into an equally damp sleeping bag. Marion followed suit, her mind's eye conjuring vortexes of rushing water. She reluctantly acknowledged the solid granite beneath her bottom as she crawled onto the thin mattress pad. Only Sammy remained with their local guide, sipping his beer, while the guide counted the dead again, resurrecting ghosts and nightwalkers out of the deep sea.

The fire glowed for a while, and then their beacon out to sea extinguished itself, leaving only dark green folds of young mountains and rocky cliffs gleaming in the subtropical moonlight.

er

And up they crawled, wet and sucking, upward past limpets locked into their calcified homes. Soggy skin scraped against sharp ridges of rock and shell. Metal dragged, a high keen on the night wind where walkers and wheelchairs jostled up the vertical cliff.

Some of these creatures of the deep left chalky marks on the cliff side: guiding lines wide enough for a car, or even, occasionally, for a wheelchair van with its unfolding flower of a side ramp.

The wind howled over the tap tap tap of a white cane tentatively reaching upward, sensing nooks beneath its nervous tip. Wind, rain and surf had carved braille patterns into the rock, enough to trace out an alternative history to the storyteller's tale of defeat and swallow. They crawled upward, relentless, unstoppable, here to stay.

When the moon emerged from behind the clouds, they had assembled on the cliff's lip. For a while, they stood sentinel, ancient statues, expressionless and looking down on the four sleepers around the dead fire. Some of them presented short silhouettes, either widened by wheelchairs or displaying limbs of unusual proportions. Others stood tall and swaying, a cane or guiding stick bristling out of their shadows. One had merged her lines with the ones of her dog, a two-headed beast now, continuous body undulating in the moon shadow. Some shivered with palsy or cold, the adrenaline of anticipation or the vibration of stimming fingers. Soft hooting drifted over the assembly, half-words, quiet commentary, a Greek chorus of long held back sounds.

et

Marion stirred first. Somehow, a chant had settled in her bones, the whispering around her sleeping place worming its way into the warmth of her dream. She stretched in her sleeping bag, her fingerless arm bulging the down-filled bag outward. Startled awake by the continuation of her dream song in the night air, she sat up.

Sammy slowly opened his eyes. His neck began its oscillation where years of psychopharmaca had eaten away at his stillness, had overwhelmed his nervous system and set it into constant waking motion. He lay as still as he could, vibrating in his sleeping bag, and listened.

Jonathan, always the most resolute of the trio, not only awoke, but pulled himself up onto his manual wheelchair, lower body still encased in the warm folds of the sleeping bag. As he swung himself powerfully upward, he took the measure of his surroundings. All around the rock place, their visitors stood side by side, encircling them. Prepared and ready to charge, he grabbed his steel guide wheels.

Only the old guide slept. He dreamt of the old days: the nursing home, secure jobs for the village, the idiots and cripples bussed in from far afield and housed in echoing corridors. He dreamt of his wife, long dead now, who had emptied bedpans and had brought home the bacon. He remembered her walking toward his car when he picked her up from the old cliffside nursing home. There was that spring in her step as she saw him and their well-polished car, her slight rush as she left behind the damp dark of the sad souls, as she walked past the poisonous conifers lining the long driveway. She hastened out into the sunlight, ready to escape to their own cozy home, their private heaven, their garden and their fireplace. Each day at six she had kissed him for his role in delivering her from the prison house of madness and despair. Every night at eight, after dinner, she had told fragmented tales of her clients—always without names, without continuation, without closure: moments of bedwetting, of straps and cannulas, of feeding tubes and of taking away crayons from defectives before their silly scrabbling would mar the wall paint again. He slept, wrapped in old dreams of old lives.

Marion, Sammy and Jonathan felt themselves melting, and hardly knew why. They looked out at the shadows surrounding them. What had smelt like piss and salt just a minute before, in the first haze of waking, registered now as the reassuring tang of tea and milky coffee. A hint of lavender and baby powder wafted from the secret places where amputated stumps met leather. The three exchanged a look. Sam signed to Jonathan, reassuring him of his watchfulness, his listening, and the fact that no words had been exchanged yet with this circle of dripping visitors.

Marion was smiling at her companions, her face wide and open, undefended, as she stretched in her skin, pushed against the skinsack that defined her, and felt it give. She rose and stood naked and without prosthesis before them, gleaming and breathing in the moonlight.

Sammy, vibrating gently, shuffled next to her, and faced out over the cliff, toward the semi-still dark figures. He breathed in, once, and felt his bones settle, his mind sending tendrils of peace to his beating heart. This is what they had come for.

Jonathan shifted the powerful muscles of his neck and shoulders, moving his steel chariot next to his friends. His strength was his pride: it allowed him access to this high cliff, allowed him to maneuver up steamy trails impassable to the power differentials of electric chairs. His leathery hands were still capable of carrying him to every mountaintop he wanted to conquer. But he had begun to feel weariness in his heart, the first fascia fibers giving notice of overwork, shoulder joints rasping in their no longer smooth hollows. So he had come.

et

The morning sun pierced through colorful clouds. The guide sat up. He was no longer surprised. His guidees had vanished: the third group in so many months. If he had had a permit it would have long been rescinded, but he provided his services well away from preying eyes. They always found him, the eager ones, ready to believe old fairytales and to pay well for a hike up to where the cliff had sheared away that raucous night so many years ago.

No one had ever followed up with him, had inquired after the disabled tourists who vanished from this tropical island paradise. The world might no longer call them defectives, fair enough. They were citizens now, and provided with ramps for their enjoyment, quiet rooms in conference centers, and talking elevators. But they still found their way to this island, now under their own steam, and they came, often in small groups, but rarely in couples, and vanished. No bodies were ever found, no tracks left behind. Who wouldn't want to dive under, lose oneself, leave the worries of the mainland behind? He didn't care, and asked for his guide money in advance.

The cave shifted in the water. Metal grated over ancient shell skeletons. It spun in the waves in its own rhythm, like the sea unlocking a portal, tumblers falling one by one.

Ruth looked through the metal round. The hem of her trousers was soaked, her shoes left safely far behind on the dry shore. She was aware that night sharks cruised not far from her position, ankle biters happy to drag her under. She stalked the metal cave carefully, avoiding the slippery canals near the break. She craned her neck. The darkness inside the portal was velvet, denser than the night sky above. There were no stars.

The object was hard to describe. She couldn't have said what size it was, if a car could have driven through, or if it could swallow her washing machine. It was big, but the vantage point necessary for comparison didn't offer itself. The silver wave's cockscomb mocked her mapping attempts.

et

The rocket had gone up two weeks ago, a red glowing dot pulsing on the Northern horizon, on its path upward toward the stars. That night, Ruth was not alone by the water. Her man stood by her, slim hand on the small of her back. Firm pressure. She complied, even out here, in public. She meant to see the rocket go up higher and arc across the sky above her. But resistance was futile, a waste of energy in which she did not wish to engage. So she let herself be pushed down by him, her body hinging at the waist, her weight landing on her palms in the cooling sand. He did not need to push her head down. She complied. She knew that his eyes were steady on the back of her head. She bowed, deeply, before the tide. The red dot, an angel flying home, had already been burned into her retina, stored and clasped. So she crouched, weight on knees and hands, head down, an animal side by side with her master. He moved up to stand by her head. Rough dark jeans over boots scuffled and scratched by the beach sand. The smell of motor oil, never far from his soft small hands. Ruth never saw his heart ride, his hog, on their sporadic dates, but she imagined him working away in a hidden garage somewhere, slim fingers gliding over chrome, leather cloth polishing a curve to high shine, till he could see himself in the machine.

That night of the rocket, time went slowly. Ruth imagined the communication satellite shifting course, stages breaking off and sailing down to earth, its rockets pointing it into a far away orbit. Then, suddenly her man stepped away, sideways and back, his hand marking with warmth a spot on the horizontal plane of her back. She stayed, obedient, as cold seeped up her arms. Each pressured grain of sand began to register in her hand's sensitive surfaces. Eventually, the tide climbed high enough to wet her fingers. With the cold touch of the midnight water came release, dissolution. She sat back on her haunches, looked around at the inky blackness of the night, and shook off the sandy crust on her palms and kneecaps. He was long gone.

A few minutes later, she found him snoring in the pick-up truck, his face squashed against the side window, mouth half open. When she climbed up in to the cab and settled herself against the passenger seat, her hand found his fist. In his sleep, he loosened, and their fingers intertwined, a small nucleus of warmth.

et

Now she had come back to the beach, alone. Past midnight again, sleep an impossibility far away, with dreams that would burn forever. She walked the shore and found the portal, the burned-through stage of the rocket, lazily drifting and circling in the waves. It had drifted here from its ocean geyser. Had it taken out any life on its long fall back to earth? An unsuspecting shark, or a stingray, hewn in two by the metal's velocity? She wondered if a shark's blood was red, and if she would see traces of it on the metal, come morning, or if the shark's death was invisible here, on the shore. She longed to touch the metal, to find out if the coldness of space shifted its molecular structure. Would it feel like familiar metal, or would it be a foreign ice, reaching back into her own marrow?

Ruth was too far into the water by now. She quickly stepped back as the salt water burned its way through the bandages that covered her lower left leg. Nerves tingled, eagerly grasping for sensations in the seedbeds of scraped skin. Ruth shivered, remembering his first touch with the whip, when her skin expanded into a field of stars. Each inch had its own exquisite specificity, fire ice burns that cried red tears on her sheets. She still had those sheets, from their first night together.

Whenever she thought of that night, back far in her mind was a small, old, crinkled celluloid image of her father whacking a wooden spoon on her naked buttocks. An image like a question mark, a thought balloon that went up and then exploded with its own weightlessness. The faded colors shifted into velvet touch and leather smoothness, when she felt the wrist bands clasp her hands, the soft leather chafing gently against her fiery skin. And then the leather thongs of the whip, each soft as a feather when he stroked her upturned face, each a rake of molten metal when it whipped across her shoulders. The touch on her nipple. The swish on her wide hips. She rocked, saltwater rushing to her.

The abandoned rocket stage reared up in front of her. On the phone not long ago, her mother had reminded her how Challenger had come down right onto the sea in front of this beach, how pieces of the tragic vessel had drifted up here for months, for years. To reach to the stars, and to know the snap of coming adrift from human time—Ruth had lain awake at night picturing what might have gone on in that little cubicle in the spacecraft among those astronauts once they knew their brief future. In her dreams the astronauts always bowed their heads, accepted the fire. She sat among them, breathing apparatus fastened over rubber mask, the rubber end firm between her teeth.

The rocket stage still emanated cold from the upper atmosphere. Ruth was very near now, and laid her hand on the dark metal. She stood up to her hips in the water.

The touch of the cool saltwater-slicked metal felt soothing. Ruth climbed into the cave. She didn't notice the sharp edge cutting into her leg, the warm rush of blood into the brine. She was tired.

℘

The night of the rocket's rise, he had woken up, eventually, had put the truck into gear. They rolled out onto the highway. He was tired, she knew that, but she trusted him. And so she slept herself, lulled by the road noise and the dispersal of the tight pose's adrenaline. Limp as a ragdoll, she survived the inferno. He hadn't. She came to as they dragged her, hands under her armpits, away from the burning truck, from the safe man, from her final command. She saw the two rows her heels made in the sand, a straight line away from his open small hand.

℘

The rocket stage whispered to her. She couldn't quite hear it. She pushed her ear against the curving wall, to a wide seam where the metal had crumpled and wrinkled upon impact. The stars hummed in her ear, a seashell hum. Whisper-kiss.

Then she pulled up her leg, astonished at the wound she found, then glad that the sharks had not come. A strip of cotton ripped from her t-shirt. Ruth bound a tourniquet, wide and solid, around her knee. She turned toward the land.

Sensory Deprivation Tank

It is smooth inside, white, with yellow edges where the light comes through. It is marine land, salty, with a hint of sweat or seaweed. You are supposed to relax, to let go. Close the pod fully, deprive yourself of all sensation, let your nervous system run amok for a few minutes before beating it, senseless, into passivity.

Yes, that was how it was to go, a bit of a letting go of our local consensual reality here in Detroit. But that is not working here. I am not working that way. There are boogeymen and too many clowns with white skin that think they can grab right in. No no baby girl. This pod stays open. Just a hint, of course, a tiny slit of orange so I know what is what, and so the air can come in. It is a bit like suffocation, you see, inside these future things. Like not enough air is coming in, and then it's all musty and wet, and my lungs scream. So here I am, bopping, yes. My ass does not touch the bottom, but I know where it is, and can touch it when I move my arm. It's cool. The salt water keeps me nicely up, and yes, the temperature is good when the air is cool enough.

"The water and the air should be the same temperature, so your body does not know which one is which."

Well, baby girl, that's all right for some of us, I guess, the full abandon in a Detroit warehouse with the sun beating down on the freeway and you wonder if your car is safe, and if it's racist to worry if it is safe, and if you do good when you carry your money to the little shop in the back alley and float, or if that is gentrification. All of that is going on, baby girl, and to breathe cool air to keep my cool is important here, so never you mind. So I float. One hour, I tell you, that is not nothing. There's the little orange light gap and the water and the air, and that's about it. Ears in water, no sound. At least not much. Maybe that's my pulse, not sure. Maybe that's the pulse of the old factory. Maybe that's a ghost breathing. Oh my, here I go again. Keep reeling it in, girl, just the facts, ma'am. I count the breaths, for a change, one and two and three and spool them spool them all the way through.

The orange seam opens up like an oyster shell. Like a midden pond, a shell circle, an old abandoned Native party scene where the pods are cracked and discarded on an ancient beach. Dinosaur legs burst the last intact ones. The time machine just keeps on flying by every fifty years or so. Last time, there were car assembly lines here, and the pods were the smooth curvy lines of General Motor chassis blocks, long curvy bodies for models to drape themselves over. These bodies got cracked, alright, with the union strike that stuck the line and kept one pod half-way off gravity's pull, suspended on steel chains, while a foreman screamed while a worker and a strike-breaker slugged it out: look at these long dinosaur tails thrashing back and forth, making a mess on the factory floor. There's still the circle on the concrete, a cipher chipped into the grey, a pentagram.

The orange seam fades out, abruptly from the slight shimmer light into full darkness. I am trying to sit up, can't. The pod's top is mere inches from my forehead, and I need to release the top to get up and out. My hands start groping. Now I hear it. Something groans right on top of the pod. Crack. Crack. There's a splinter spider. There's a hairline starlight brilliance. There's a crack. Something shifts, right on top, right fully on top of this old plastic thing, and I think to myself, wow, something is sitting there, something big and heavy, warty, stinky, something like a swamp creature, another dinosaur, this time the time machine didn't stop in time and went all around the dial and back and back and back.

I breathe, try to calm down and not make a move or a sound. The tiny cracks right above my face are not orange with the outside light. They are a slight red, like there is not quite enough sun out there to warm up their edges, to send the fullness of light through the plastic capillaries. Murky. Maybe riot gas drifts like urban fog through the factory, men in face-shields too afraid of black skin to do anything but suit up and armor, gun at the ready and oh my god my pod is right in the line right in the shooting alley right there in the crack.

The crack hasn't widened at all. It's a dusty canopy now, a star map, lines of zodiac assemblages sketched out between principle stars. I am in an observatory, learning about the planets and the universe. The crack glistens, little diode pearls harvested from tiny child labor fingers from far-away factories, set like crown jewels in the old dome. I listen to the commentator, some forgettable music wafting between words.

"This is what the sky would look like if there were no city lights, no street lights, nothing to pollute our eyes."

I am thinking, that's like Detroit now then, no street lights, see where you are going with that, university man, to the places where we can name the city by the avenues of the stars. There are the Motown singers, babes and deep bass sounds to rock your spine. The music between the stars changes, shifts. Percussion and the sax drill deeper through the cracks into the waters that hold my soggy skin. I feel the beat against my back the beat the beat the heart the drum the heart.

Painting the Asylum Garden

"A view of the garden of the asylum where I am, on the right a
gray terrace; on the left, the earth of the garden—red ochre—
earth burnt by the sun, covered in fallen pine twigs."

"You'll understand that this combination of red ochre, of
green saddened with grey, of black lines that define the outlines, this gives rise a little to the feeling of anxiety from which
some of my companions in misfortune often suffer, and which
is called 'seeing red'."

VINCENT VAN GOGH,
in a letter about his painting to Émile Bernard

I am caught in paint. Thick purples and blues touching cad-
mium orange. Cobalt and lead white streak over my ankles
and wrists. The painting is from 1889. You'd think it'd be dry
by now. But no, it still flows, still expands downward with the
pull of gravity. Vincent has done his level best to not be alone.
He has me, now. To be precise, "Garden at the Asylum Saint
Paul Hospital" has me like honey had the fly on the café cup
and saucer yesterday, in the Oslo town square of Lille Toyen, in
Norway, melancholy city.

All around me, functionaries' mellow stone buildings
soared, the old offices and living quarters of the social security administration, now privatized into little coffin blocks for
square families. Baby strollers everywhere. And in the middle
of it, I, at the café table, drinking a soy latte and getting stuck. I
wasn't stuck then, of course: I was just walking, strolling, a fla-
neur in streets that had held open their cupped palms for over
a hundred years, uncanny invitations of at-home-ness encoded
in well-restored shutters, thresholds, and curtain rods. After I
downed my latte, I had wandered away again, slouching past
the honeyed stone as if looking for a household cat to drain of
its meager blood.

It was only later that night, in the privacy of my apartment, that I found my way into the paint.

It had lain there, curious, inviting. A thick artist's book on asylums and their visual histories. Who wouldn't look? Who would not follow a troll down the avenue of perfectly trimmed plane trees, down the straight line of a drive, to the mansion that only sometimes cackled with manic laughter? You would have looked, too, attracted by your memories of weird Psycho films and the appeal of psychopharmaca, for you, too, want to know how it feels to peel sleek cling-film over the multi-lobed valleys of your brain.

Shut the window, bar the door. Vincent had gone to the Saint-Remy hospital gardens to visit, to recuperate, to get well. I was travelling to write, to think about international disability culture, to connect with those who turn away from their doctors' words for their brain shift. I search for fellows to slant against the hale apple trees.

In the coffee table book mellow threat leeches into asylum reclamations. That was then, the foreword says. There, the ordered lines, the patients tucked away, or locked, in the harmony of the garden. And where are we now. Asylum seekers clamoring to be let in let in let in. Their faces dour with the pain of leave-taking. Prowl, if you will, but the asylum doors shut closer and closer and pinch into black.

So, yesterday night, I opened the book, bored with my own writing as another bomb explodes somewhere, limbs fly halfway around the world to stick in the web. Exhausted and bored with the vista of no date, no contact, the self-imposed deadlines of a scribbler's life.

Then I had brushed a hand lightly against the book's page, as if stroking it flat into my life, and the lead white oil paint had risen to my hand and felt warm and squishy like a woman's breast. The red vermillion had beckoned with little globules of red lead. I dove in, then, fingers trailing and following the lines that up close did not resemble any tree, any earth, any border. Here, my nose to the smell of turpentine, the whiff of oils, I had tumbled into the French ultramarine as the shadows gathered on the outlines of the tree limbs that suddenly became the backs of people, walking, the hands of fellow inmates, raised high in the air as if saluting a swallow that sails, dot dot dot, toward a barn none of us can see but that segments the sky with every downbeat of her feathered wings.

The mud of the far side of the painting felt even warmer to my fingers, the small of my back, my pelvis dissolving into the wide open page. Like a thermal pool heated to envelop a human form, let it sweat and dissolve the salty residues of tears back into the linen earth. I spread into the black streaks of the wandering man, black, the end. He wandered canvas and gloss, lost, tiny against the onslaught of white flowers leaning threateningly toward him, a reddish earth opening under his feet. I wished to unglue, but it was too late, much too late, and the oils and the heavy metals crept closer, closer, as the sky lowered itself, as the windows shut tight, as I wallowed, wallowed in the cerulean wave sky, blood red pulse earth, till Vincent stopped me and bathed me in his viscous liquids. I bled then, blood streaming down the side of my face and mingling with the paint, pricked for good in framed perspective.

III: WAVES

The Road under the Bay

Long ago, reaching out up here on the bridge, my hand on the hammer, a workman's hammer, solid and heavy. The bottom edge is rusty in the salty winds, but my palm has kept the shaft smooth and warm, a winking eye in the sun. I heave forward. The hammer shines. My boot slips. The other. Water rushes up. My eyes are open, looking down at the blinding ripples, as the net beneath the bridge pushes the air out of me, and I bounce back up. I crest, past the rivets, and fall again. There: the twang of the metal spirals giving way, the crack, recoil, decay. All happens so fast. I slide and scrape along the undulating net, my hands grasping, useless. The second bounce does not come. I just fall.

The shocking coldness of the water. The deep bend in my spine as I go under and my limbs drive up from my torso. A jellyfish's mantle beating down, up, down, up, down. A flash of grey. There's the shark who has waited beneath the net all these months. I had looked down on you, shark, spit into the blue-grey waves, tried to hit your tiny snub-nosed head from high up in the bridge's fiber work. Now, your teeth fall like a hammer. Around me, crimson.

Now. So many nows. I am floating here, waiting. I stand here, beneath my Golden Gate, the entry to this promised future. The rivets I've driven are now bleeding red into the ocean. We are all standing here, awaiting our reward, so many of us workers, fallen off the red girders, crushed on the black ocean, buried in the grey slush of memory and the sickness of sea passages. The cars above weave a vibrating cage of iron and concrete. The sea symphony keeps me here. I shall not pass over. My spine is a spongy weed. All my nows are down here now, and will ever be. My wages are still waiting to be paid. I shall have my recompense, my promised land, a warm bed.

et

Far across from the red bride and its deep shadows, Doris has entered the Bay's waters. Her foot tasted the cool salty liquid, almost slipped on the algae-covered rocks. She rebalanced, checked behind her that no-one observed her first attempt at entry. The stone wall at Point Isobel rose placid and quiet to her left, and no dog bounded down the access stairs. No one panicked, seeing her entry. Good.

She had chosen the right time, between the morning professional dog walkers and the late afternoon crowd. The sun was high, but didn't yet reflect off the neon-green wind-breakers of people she'd seen here for months now, with whom she had never spoken a word. No one had asked which dog was hers. For weeks she had been a boulder on the edge of the path, something dogs and walkers careened around. It had been pleasant, leaning out over the breakwater, with the tang of the ocean in the wind, her hair tousled by the breezes that lifted the stink of too much dog shit. Her hour of escape after spending her days filing ship manifests for large oceangoing tankers. Pleasant, and enough, for many years.

But today, there had been the albatross outside her office. It had stood on its legs, large and lumpy, staring up at her window. Doris had stopped as she got up from her desk, one hand full of papers, ship manifests to be checked and tabulated. The other hand had smoothed aside the grey silk curtains that kept the world at bay. There was the bird. What was it doing here?

She had seen many sea birds flying high above the rocks by the shore, their silhouettes diving in and out of the wave hollows, or standing still and pecking at the asphalt of the coastal path. But an albatross? She could not remember such a giant bird wheeling among them, and surely none had ever been here in the yard outside her office building, not among these box topiary and tulips that wouldn't withstand one nip of the blow of the Bay.

Doris hadn't moved. Through the thick sheet of glass the large white creature stared right back at her, unswayed. The spreadsheets of cargo loads fell from her hand, papers feathering out and intermingling.

She had held the albatross's stare. Then Doris had raised the water glass and had begun pouring water onto her desk, the sound of dripping and splashing barely reaching her ears. Eventually, she had looked away from the dark globes of the bird's eyes. Shock ran through her as she saw the destroyed papers on her desk. Red and blue ink flowered across the regular black lines, flowed until they met in the polished depth of the mahogany captain's desk.

Something had shifted, in that silent invitation of the albatross's eyes. From one moment to the next, the tankers' loads had sunk out of sight. Her own body longed for the deep water. Doris ached for pressure and silence.

Another step down the coastal stairway.

The bottoms of her suede trouser legs floated up, turned over. She smiled as she felt the sweet clasp of density on her ankle. She could no longer see the rough steps in the dense sea, and found her way down by touch. Another few moments, and she floated free from all stone. The Golden Gate stood sentinel far out on the Western horizon.

Doris floated horizontally, lolled by small choppy waves. Then she breathed out and sank. The debris already accumulating around her stayed at the surface. She didn't sink far, for this part of the Bay was shallow and filthy with coastal mixing. Just far enough for her limbs to remember swimming without effort.

She shot out into the green. At the near bottom, the stones snaked their way from Point Judith's staircase westward across the Bay. She followed, hovering along. For the first few minutes she felt compelled to return to the surface, holding less breath each time.

At her last surfacing, beneath the weak sun, her eyes blinked away the slight sting of salt, effluvia, and jet fuel. Without holding her breath, she dove again, followed the long dark road that led to the place beneath the bridge.

ℰ

I can feel the change. The nows, assembling, limning onto each other, old memories and new ripples. Standing here, waiting, I can feel it in the ancient water. Salts, pressure, the way the sound drives through the ocean—somewhere nearby, something has changed, and has changed for me. Someone is coming, and it is my turn to lay claim. She is coming. I have stood here, in the half darkness, till my bones crumbled and fused, till seaweed lacerated the remains of my clothes, till all mingled, fluids to fluids, and whatever was solid corroded away.

This one is coming from the East, not from the bridge above. She is coming through the waters. This one is coming, and she is for me.

The blue roars, shifts, the deep waves of the ocean reaching back to the Farralon Islands and the Great Whites' mating grounds. I remember the stories. Fast shadows circle me. To my right, a row of sharp teeth wink in the murky light. They are with me, the sharks, night and day, and our purpose has become one: to mate, and to endure.

I lean just so, break the cage of electric lines, conduct the hum into the water, a beacon, a lure.

ℰ

His hum reaches forward, eastward, spreads out like a darker stain in the dark waters. The sharks retreat out into the blue, driven away by the keening. The sound ripples out, and eventually, its outer edge reaches Doris, still on her way, half-way across the Bay by now, her lungs filled with saltwater. The sound embraces her, pulls her along.

Doris remembers the sound.

"Mum, my teeth are hurting!"

"It's your people calling, little one, a reminder of home. All the love, and all the promise, over the sea and beyond the stars." Her mother, clad in an oyster-color silk shift, had freshly returned from a night out in the small town of Bar Harbor. The strange low-level hum hadn't stopped, and Mum handed her a lemon to bite into.

"When will it stop, Mum? It hurts!"

"I feel it, too, Doree, I know. Just don't bite down on your teeth, leave them open a bit. It'll help. Don't spit: the water in your mouth will help, it will dim the vibrations."

"When will it stop?"

"Soon, babe, soon." And her mother had crooned, holding her close, Doris's face pressed into the slippery coolness of the mother's gown, her small hand holding long fingers. Her mother had distracted her by working loose a small ring from her own finger, a thin silver band, with an aquamarine cut into a square.

"Here, babe, play with that. See that stone? See deep inside? That's where they live, far away and under the sea, all the ones we've lost, that's where they live, and one day, maybe, you can visit with them."

The ring became her childhood companion, and she knew its story, given to her mother by Doris's father, a fisherman lost in the sea.

Now, deep under the sea, Doris's head is full with the humming, now a much deeper pitch in the colder salty waters of the Pacific. Doris's thumb reaches out to her little finger, and touches the silver band, the aquamarine jewel, so much smaller now in her hand than that night when she first slipped it onto her thumb, so much more fragile. She remembers being held, being caressed, the cool sweetness of her mother's embrace.

She has not seen her mother for many years. One week after the first time Doris had heard this hum, her mother had vanished, had gone down in her oyster silk to the ocean's edge, had stood in the moonlight, listening, and had waded in. Doris had watched, not knowing her mother's intention. As an adult Doris had never forgiven herself for not knowing what was happening, for not stopping her mother. Surely her sleek mother was just going swimming, in a warm summer night, in a dress that transformed in the moonlight to a wet shark's leather, to a pearly diver's skin.

The hum had ended, that night. And now here it is, again, with the memory of silk and hair and caress. She feels the same pull she had sensed from the albatross and his staring eyes. Longing for her new brethren, she swims on. With each undulation of her swimming limbs, there are the wide wings of the albatross, opening for her.

et

I do not know her shape. It does not matter, not anymore, hasn't mattered for a long time. I feel my workman's promise, bright and clean as the hammer's shaft, in the watery coils of what was once my brain, where I once thought, all by myself, of love and sheets and hot toddies. She will arrive, she will comfort me, she and I will build a home, on the rim, by the beach. We will be one.

Flashes, like a strike of the sun on the blue sea. Other nows. I remember. The man with a black hat signing me up in our small village in Italy, the hot sun on baked stone, the smell of jasmine. I had bargained, like a dutiful son, for ship passes for my widowed mother and me. I climbed onto the big ship, to go out and build a new bridge in a new land. Yes, the long journey, seasickness, the rain. Arrival: the ship coming into port, through this opening between the rocky coasts, the opening unguarded by lengthening land arms.

To feel the land again beneath my boots. This new earth, clammy, and foggy. On the wharf, my old mother on my arm, I heard the rumor, an answering moan from us young men, men from the Old Country, men who had been good, who had been honorable. Immigration had closed down, no more Italians, no permits, no fiancée between the damp bedsheets. I nearly fell, and it was my mother who held me upright that day.

At night there's the sound of the accordion drifting over from the tavern, climbing up the wooden side of our boarding house. When my mother went to sleep, I turned to the wall. My prick erect, I cried and cried, my heart adrift with the sound across the water, through the fog, to the sharks in the Bay who circle and breed and never stop.

The promise of the bridge is still here. I am still here. The promise runs in the water, and it boils in me, now. I am holding on to the promise, like my fellows down here in the water shadow, lined up here, awaiting our reward. She is coming, and I will have her. My lover, mine, my union.

et

The transformation is complete. Doris's body has found its rhythm. She glides along the road under the Bay, still on her trajectory toward the bridge. The two deep stone supports emerge on her vision's horizon. Nearly there.

Her tissues are changing. Salt crystals flood her blood, thin it, transform it, each molecule in its own dance of adaptation and exchange. Delicate barriers breach, water expands cell shunts, floods compartments. She does not know how to pay attention to the minuteness of her changing world, but she knows the roil deep inside her. DNA strands unweave and re-weave, a mitosis of a new embrace. Small cytoplankton organisms wander in, and find their home in new pools, rooting deep through her flesh. Cells burst gently, opening like flowers. Tiny fragments of mitochondria unspool and align themselves with the sticky ends of Doris's older strands, new pearl strings clicking into place.

Between her fingers, thin membranes uncoil forward toward tender tips. Liquids wash embryotic growth nubs, skins push forward and fill the space between the fingers. Sensations change, and Doris can feel salinity and electric currents in new, exhilarating ways. She moves forward.

Doris' speed doubles, the newly webbed fingers more adept at pushing her toward the shadows that she can now see, first a line of grey, and then differentiated, one by one, a long column of shapes stretched out below the monstrous bridge. Which one?

A last moment of doubt runs through Doris, a hesitation. She is drawn forward—but is it right? Is this the call? The doubt vanishes in a final wave of hormones. There—a copper flash in the line, a hammer raised high, skeletal mélange of bones and weeds arcing up, triumphant. She hones in. That one. That one. Let it be the one.

et

Doris arrives. Her face is gone now, swept aside and upward, replaced by a silvery caul. The exultation of arrival engulfs the last fragments of memory, of Atlantic beaches, of river dates and diving expeditions. For one moment, what remains of her finger touches a thin silver band, half worked through the spongy remnant of bone.

Collision.

The aquamarine jewel flashes from the deep, a small blue-silver edge shoots out of the water, toward the red steel ropes above. It reflects, for a second, off a red Prius's windshield. The driver does not notice, lost in the contemplation of the smooth sea. A kestrel notices, circling through the steel ropes that striate the sky, and adjusts his flight.

"Lover," someone thinks, a she in a moment of now. "Lover," someone replies, a he in a moment of now. The ring loosens, and drifts down toward the ocean floor, to the clearing that forms the terminus of the long road. The silver settles, winks, and vanishes in the folds of an old work boot, a skeleton of leather and metal hobnails.

River Crossing

She looked at Dana, saw the moon and the sun in her wide belly, the low-slung breasts. A bumblebee landed on Dana's shoulder, buzzed, the blurred wings beating on the lines of Dana's old skin. Sun dithered across ditches. Solange felt tears prickling her eyes. She witnessed Dana's dance.

Once, maybe six years ago, the local tavern had organized a dance in the square to raise money for a local orphanage, and Solange and Dana had been part of the long line that Cotton-Eye Joe'd in boots and jeans. Here was another dance, now, naked, vulnerable, in the dust of the highway, with some dried-up orange rinds left over from Wednesday's Farmers Market. The rinds looked like Butoh powder beneath Dana's feet, stomped into fine meal. The feet were cracked, with long elder nails and a crooked left toe.

Solange knew the story of the crook, the twist story of a fall over an aircraft door, Albuquerque airport, a cowboy boot stuck in the open seam between the jet bridge and the plane. Dana, then in her thirties, going down like a sack of potatoes. Solange remembered laughing when Dana had told the story, explaining the limp that accompanied her barrel voice and rotund body. Later that night, Solange had probed that story for cracks, had imagined the embarrassment of someone no longer quite young exposing herself in the airport, help rushing in, the warding off of touching hands by a person who did not feel fine in her skin, who wasn't well, and who'd rather limp than let a doctor set her foot.

Here was Dana now, full thirty years on, dancing her last public dance in the town square, or what used to be a town square when they had more than a weekly farmers market, when there were rodeos and cattle round-ups, men prancing in spurred boots, their gear clanging in the air.

Solange was rooted, watching. Dana crouched down, touched her feet, shifted her weight from the achy-toed-foot to the other one. Let her weight rest on her knees, a folded bundle. Then she stretched upward, let her palms run up the side of her sagging belly, lifting and gently dropping the fullness, moving up to the soft skin of her breasts, each gingerly cradled in a palm, their nipples erect in the cooling desert air and the stare of the audience.

Solange was not the only one witnessing Dana's homecoming. The town square was filling now. The bar emptied into a raucous sidewalk. A bang: the first beer bottle crashed, shards exploding across the plaza. Dana's naked feet looked precarious now.

Anything could happen as the sun sank, drowned in the Rio Grande. Did Dana feel the danger? Solange wasn't certain, and wrapped her arms around herself as her lover inched backward, stepped carefully. At last Dana turned. The full moon of her backside was white in the last orange light. It shone with the whiteness of purity, dough for heavenly meals. Above it, the skin darkened in a cowboy's tan, sun-dark like oil running into old creases. But the moon shone on, wobbled as Dana stepped forward into the river that hugged the town like a snake asleep in the early fall.

The river was as calm as it got, only slight turbulences marking its swift passage. Dana's foot entered and her calf followed, the thigh, the moon of her ass, the water creeping up the tattoo on her back. A snake shifted in the fading light. It was black on her skin, a desperate rattler caught in the jaws of a border river.

Solange remembered her fingers tracing that tattoo, the two of them curled like spooning kittens beneath the quilt, softness and sleep breath.

On the far river side, sharp shooters stood like silhouettes in the night. The first one raised a gun toward the watery moon goddess.

et

Dana swam in the river. On the other side were border guards. She knew the danger. She knew what they were seeing: another wetback, white body, larger than most, trying to muscle in on territory that was now forbidden by the unfair laws of birth and nationhood. She also knew that her love for Solange would not find favor with the brown man who held passports interminably in grey cubicle rooms with warning signs at head height, making up with procedure for decades and centuries of other border stories. There was no wall, not yet. But there were the sharp shooters incensed by wars of attrition, by children dying in deserts, by a world that let coyotes thrive. Dana knew all that, and yet she gave herself gladly to the red waves. The snake on her back went under, settled horizontally. No crack yet, no pinpoint of light on her wet webbed skin. Behind her, she could hear Solange crying.

Soon, babe, soon. The dreams told us that we can only go one by one. Soon. This is my time, my blood time. We all have to face this alone.

Dana dove.

Beneath her, the red river went dark. The world of the air split off, sounds attenuated, explosions and laughter long gone behind her. She extended her arms, powerful muscles driving down. Alongside, a tiny salamander dove with her, its yellow pearl patches gleaming. They shimmered in the remaining half-light, golden and warm. They pulled her on. Her lungs began to ache already, a bit too early, but still on the edge. She could do this. She pulled, down, down, waves of fat insulating her against the bottom cold. Her legs were strong, the land limp long forgotten. There it was: the hole in the river.

They had let her through. No red warmth bled into the river from her exposed back. No one shot her. She was fast and sure at this outer edge of her body's ability. She pushed through the hole, one last swipe of arms and legs, and then her feet vanished into the darkness.

𝓮𝓽

Solange sat by the river edge. The sharp shooters had lowered their weapons. No one emerged at their side of the river, and no one had endeavored to do so, either. She knew Dana's goal, of course. But that did not make it any easier.

Bye, beloved. Bye for now, bye for how long. Who will know.

Solange did not believe in goddesses, but she traced her hand in the river as if calling on ghosts and protection. Behind her, the town dispersed. Nothing to see here. A naked big woman had danced herself to her death. Not exactly a daily occurrence, but often enough, no longer the spectacle of sacrifice that it was when Kim, Mara, Judy and Nick first went ahead and made their river passage, drawn by old stories of a world beyond this one, on the other side of the big river, for those strong enough to reach it. Dana was the end of the line, for now. Solange would have to wait, to train more, to hold her breath in the bathtub longer and push bigger weights in the gym. Eventually they would all be together again. Wouldn't they?

𝓮𝓽

Dana's lungs were exploding. The beads of tender whiteness spasmed in her chest, forced her to open her mouth, to gasp water or air. What would it be? She put on a last spurt of effort, push, push, willing herself out of the hole. Then there was light. A change of pressure. Something. She opened her eyes and opened her throat at the same time.

Kim emerged first from behind the veils. She sat upright, muscular legs drawn under her on the bed. Brocade and silks, luscious maroon and oranges, highlights like the salamander's

125

yellow. A four-poster bed. Kim had dusted eye shadow over her upper lids, heavy and hanging down on the left, a remnant of a dust-up outside a saloon that wouldn't support its rainbow flag window in deed. That night Kim had lost the facial symmetry that had made her so proud. They all saw it, Mara and Judy, her beloved Nick, Dana and Solange, as they gathered the next day in the broken-down parlor. No hospital for Kim, no, too dangerous, from the intake interview to the insurance forms. That night, red blood mixed with the lacquer of defiant pinks, smoothed over cupid bows. Kim shifted her relationship to make-up, to the jewels of her mother's color box, so long out of reach for the little boy-girl with the delicate hands. Now the make-up had become war-paint, a new bravado in the peacock colors dusting high cheek bones. Darkness masked the beginning of a widow's peak, eyebrow pencil to gunpowder.

Kim had been the first to leave nothing but a trail of bubbles in the river, shimmering orbs, petrol swirls glistening for a long time before they burst down river, where kids threw sticks at otters.

One of these bubbles had opened now, for Dana. She pressed her naked snake back against its curve. The bed reared in the darkness, Kim on it like a sailor in a storm, the brocade in tatters, then intact, moth-eaten, water-logged, then pretty and starched lace like a show room display. Dana tried to blink, but knew that her bubble depended on the love in her gaze. She felt her eyes drying. The bubble shimmered, shivered, a long sigh escaped from the bed, a languid caress from a mouth blood red and fire engine red and stop sign red and now it formed itself into a lionfish's thick rich lips, yellow and red and they gulped.

Nick blinked at her, brown eyes hidden in the foliage of the bed's paladin, silk fringes coming down into his hair, brown blond and dishy. Dana remembered the hair dryer in Kim and Nick's apartment. It was plugged in, purple fingers extending from a heat-diffusing plate, ready to shift curls into planes of wavy delight. One night Dana and Solange had played with the monster, had pressed it against their own hair until they smelled the singe in the bathroom. Kim, laughing, had asked them to pack it in.

She remembered when Nick had followed Kim into the river, remembered the day ten years ago, a special day, when Nick had baked cake for them all. White frosting, silver doves, a wedding cake that crumbled just a tad dry under their forks as Nick hadn't known to put in enough eggs. His first, he said proudly, tears far back in the hollows of his eyes.

They hadn't known yet that there was the river cave hollow. Those dreams had started later, when things got even harder, when the town came for more and more of them, more often, became even less accountable to the law. Ten years ago, none of the lovers had known that they could come when their bodies were ready for transition. So that night of Nick's cake, they had all just said good-bye, cried a bit, left the yellow warmth of the house one by one, never in couples. They knew that pick-up trucks might be standing guard down the road, by the bar, some folks always ready to pick out the wrong two-by-twos. So they had left in separate trucks, cars, motorbikes, curving a lonely road down to tucked away driveways.

et

Kim, and Nick. Then the dreams had started for the rest of them, and they were all so eager for instructions, for ideas to get them out, to find a new, more fluid world. So Mara followed Kim and Nick into the river, then Judy, now Dana. Solange remained, her head full of protective rituals of strength, her heart singing a dirge. She picked up the orange rind from the dusty square. She dropped it into the river, saw the salamander come up, nibble, retreat, come forward again. No shot, but no ambulance, either. No one spoke to her. The show was long over.

Without social security, pension rights, human status, there was nothing much to say if one of them dropped over edges, let go of the water's rim, and kissed the fishes.

The town had gone to sleep. If some had plans to approach her by the river's edge, they looked at her hunched shoulders, listened to the hitch in her breath, and some tiny mercy remained.

Solange stayed by the river for hours. Under the full moon, in the darkness of owl eyes, she dropped into plank pose, push-ups, till the small of her back cracked, till her knee came down hard on a rock. Then she waited, gulped down the bitter taste of defeat, felt the copper rising, and started again, counting to one hundred, felt the blood flow through her veins.

Fjord Pool

The fjord city clasped the shiny rim of the pool at night. A troll pool, designed for large flat-footed creatures with curly hair. The hallway from the showers to the pool is empty and dark. Set into the hallway walls are round observation windows, full of blue light: the pool from beneath, tunnels to see the swimmer creatures on their lines, beetles webbing their way across black bars and blue waves.

In the nascent blue sheen of night, the trolls come out. They roll down the hill, over the mountain, dip into oily lakes deep beneath the crust. They shake their matted hair in the fjords, mini tsunamis worrying widows in their coastal huts. They climb into the 50-meter pool of Toyen Badet, Oslo's public bath, and launch themselves cross-wise against the lengths, jump high and land on their bellies, laugh at the tickle and dunk down.

Astrid remembered her aunt telling her troll stories, when they had sat side by side in the kiddie pool. Her aunt had her legs drawn up under her, kneeling lightly in the warm water. Astrid had jumped up and down, the water still reaching under her armpit. She must have been five, then, or younger. Now, she still sat in the warm pool at the end of her lengths, and let her legs float out under her. The shimmer of the water was cut by the diagonal of the ramped entry way, a collage of angles and lines converging. Its angularity pleased Astrid's eye.

Her auntie had held her up to the blue holes in the walkway below the pool, and they had stared, together, at the swimmers, at the light, at the magic of observation itself. And later, Astrid had seen televised swim events from this pool, saw again the magic round underwater eyes capturing graceful landings of jumpers, the entry of bubbles and splash. The perspective made her cry, stifle a little sob, and then she remembered her aunt's stories of trolls and other mountainfolk going for a swim.

She cupped a handful of water, let it run out over her knees, warming the cooling flesh. Today, she had to decide about the operation. Would she give up these hillocks sprouting on her chest? She squeezed her hill country between her upper arms. Familiar, and ticklish: not at all dangerous, riven with deep secrets, probed and biopsied. She could go full hog, radical clear-cutting, or decide to go with the lumpy story, the bits and pieces. Hours before she saw her doctor, and her mind still wasn't made up.

She launched herself sideways in the kiddie pool, let gravity take over her body's trajectory in the shallow water. She twirled, twisted, felt the tug of skin where skin's elastic offered counter-pull. The glory of her treasure, her hoard. Astrid whispered to herself the troll secrets, the jewels under the hills.

Beneath her, the seams of tile fluctuated, small streams of bubbles heating under a dragon's breath. Astrid kept twirling, shooting sideways, feeling the strength of her leg muscles, thighs powerful like small horses. Each time her feet punched into the tiles, a little bit more gave, a crack of opening, dilation. She still hadn't noticed the changes on the pool floor. The clock kept ticking.

Her aunt, no longer able to pull her legs beneath her. Unstable. The awkwardness of the bath chair, rolling down the kiddie pool ramp. For a while, they could still go to the public bath together. Then, her aunt's skin had cracked, continents adrift in dry lost deserts. After that, her mind had leaked, gone fuzzy at the edges, in ways that a teenager could only find frighteningly unclear. Astrid wondered about how she would know her aunt's story now, with her own feet anchored firmly in the world.

Astrid dolphin-ducked her way across the shallow warm pool, her back's muscles lifting and arcing her through the waters. Her mind's eye was still far in the past, so she didn't notice the buckling of the tiles in rhythm with her own undulation.

Then she turned, and floated on her back, aware of her breasts spreading out over her chest, spilling like warm dough over the sides. The same, and separate: she already was taking so much more note of these skin sensations, the little feedback from gravity and posture, stuff that would have been far in her unconscious even as recently as two weeks ago. Bodies change. She seal-rolled, side, side, side, side, shift, lift, flutter.

The pool floor erupted beneath her. A pressure wave moved her sideways, pitched her into an eskimo-roll. She handled it fine, her body feeling no need to panic, just a duck and weave, then upward. Her head broke through the warm water, and she looked around, alert, her fear catching up with her diaphragm. She hiccupped and stared. In the middle of the shallow kiddie pool at Toyen Badet, a troll had taken up residency. She, for she seemed feminine, was hairy all over, with slightly chlorinated water now dripping clear out of her fur—no mud on this gal. The hair was shiny and looked soft, and it draped her generous body in waves and folds. A giant nose peeked out of a waterfall of locks. She blew through thick rosy lips, and the hair rose upward as if on a giant hairdryer, floated, and then blew over her head, cascading downward again. Now the nose was freed and it shone even more rosy in the middle of multiple folds, a face wrinkled and strangely young-old. Astrid found it hard to hold on to any fear or even consternation. The troll looked friendly, cheeky, maybe mischievous, but hardly malevolent. She unglued her booty from the pool floor, and duck-eeled her way over to the giant.

The giant responded, elegantly swishing a large hand through the water, as if tracing Astrid's outline. Astrid, in turn, ducked under and planed like an arrow through the blue. The water was a bit higher now, as the troll had displaced quite a bit, and seemed to be blocking with her ass any outflow. This was more fun! Astrid banked, breathed, and went under again, slingshooting off the troll's back pelt. The troll leaned back, into the wave created by Astrid's cresting form. The troll opened her mouth, and laughed. The far distant concrete ceiling shook in response vibration, but held safe and firm. The troll let herself fall back, so the water created a rim all around her. Astrid swam this ring, darting in and out of the fjords of the troll's dark brown soft and undulating body.

So they played, water mediating between them, large and small, mountain and salmon. Eventually, Astrid tired, and the troll held out a large lined hand. Astrid crawled inside, rolled up, and the troll blew on her, drying her, breath strangely sweet and smelling of salmiak licorice. Then the troll deloused her. At least that is how it felt to Astrid, lying still. As the procedure unfolded, she began to hold herself in a ball a bit more stiffly, for some inkling of danger made its way through the layers of curled child pleasures that engulfed her. Large horny nails shifted Astrid's folds and valleys, plucked her bathing suit right off her, tearing and discarding the bits. Astrid looked over the hand's rim, saw the purple flakes of suit rain down a long way to the pool's surface. Then the horned pincers returned.

Night fell over the pool. Far down, on Oslo Fjord, a large cruise-ship cast off its lines, and headed out into the darkening sound, a lowing ship's horn blast echoing across the harbor. Astrid awoke, stiff and cold on hard tile. What had happened? She was shivering, and found herself naked underneath her sheltering hands. Her skin felt raw in places, scabby even, as if she had been dragged behind a truck over a country road. She welled those fears: she was still in the pool building, safe, and breathing. She was also alone. The troll had gone. In front of her, the kiddie pool lay placid and still. She stood up, stacked her vertebrae one on top of the other, found all muscles responding and willing, if creaking. She walked to the main pool, and looked down into the clear water. The round observation globes in the depth glowed gently back at her, shimmering. She tested the main pool with her toes: colder than the kiddie pool, but acceptable to her achy chill self. She looked around once more. No one was here. None of it made sense. Astrid laughed, head thrown back, with the moon high above Toyen Pool, shining on fjord, city, and mountain.

She jumped in, and cold blue water engulfed her, swirled around her, entered each pore and probed each entry into her form. She twirled in the water, swam down to the light globe, and glided like an elf through the silver blue lights. She opened and closed her eyes in the water, silver membranes shielding her pupils. She flexed her hands, felt the webbing between the finger joints, and felt the speed. Cartwheel, duck weave, eel ride.

Pool Shark

Gaby let go of the green tile, pushing herself into the end-less space behind. She didn't look, dared herself not to look. Instead, she floated, the back of her shoulders itchy with a worry she could not suppress. The water beneath her felt cold-er than the water surrounding her. She knew she was paddling out into the deep. Out of the corner of her eyes she saw the pearls of the dividing lines change color, from white to orange, marking the point where the pool floor dropped down, down, ever deeper into murkiness.

Gaby breathed once, twice, and then threw herself forward, arms frantically throwing water behind her, till she gained the safety of the white pearls again. She angled to the wall and clung to the drain, her hand wedged into the space of the float-ing hairs. She panted into the well, the smell of chlorine min-gling with the copper of adrenaline. Her back to the pool, to the others, to whoever might be watching her, and pointing at her. She looked straight ahead, at the grout between the tiles, the thin white line that ran steady and unbroken between the shiny bits. Breathing.

Later, nearly dry under the July sun, Gaby decided it was time to return to her towel in the far field, and she wasn't going to take the long way around. She breathed. She knew she had to face them, again, and that it had to be done, or they would get her on the way home.

Dave and Jim saw her first. She placed one foot after the oth-er on the crack between the large concrete tiles, giving herself a line. Head down, just a bit, just to anchor to the line. Just a few steps. She walked.

"Hey dumbass." Dave.

"Hey fatface." Jim.

They sounded bored. Maybe good? Maybe too lazy to do

anything but call out? Gaby walked on, on one side the deep end of the pool, on the other the two boys on their blankets.

One of them got up. She tried to speed up, but her legs were frozen, each drop of water turning to ice on her skin, and she had to break each step through sheets of congealing terror. Oh no. No. Jim was coming at her. Gaby couldn't think. She was too near to the pool's edge, to the deep end, to the darkness below and too far from the white and the green of the towels and the grass, and she just could not move fast enough... Jim was there, now.

He didn't look menacing, he looked nice, even, blond fried to white in the summer, like the drummer she liked in the band. But he wasn't nice, not nice at all: he didn't say much, just got to her, big and then bigger, and a hand was out, and he shoved, with a sudden emphasis she hadn't expected, or maybe her legs would have unfrozen themselves, unlocked from the icy embrace of the concrete path that had turned into Antarctica.

But the legs hadn't.

She was nearly standing still when he lifted her with his giant push, both feet leaving the tiles, and her arms didn't move from her sides, still pinned down in terror, as she sailed over the edge. She had time to look down, to look into the murkiness of the deep end, and it was all true, all true, and it was coming at her, from beneath, having sensed her entry here. It was coming up.

Gaby felt relief, so strange, for not having been told a lie, to know for sure that it did live here and did come and get you. For there it was.

The shark rose toward her as she hit the water, the giant maw wide like a car. She fell past the teeth, not a hair touched by the ivory spears. No drop of water reached her, either, as she tumbled down a dark red gullet. Then she touched the side, cool, and felt herself turned around.

Above her, she could still see the terrifying teeth, still moving forward with the shark's momentum out of the pool, and she could see Jim, his eyes unbelieving and white, caught on the pool's edge. The shark's teeth slid through him like warm butter knives. Gaby heard a sound like a sausage skin bursting on the grill, and felt a warm shower, Jim's blood, raining down into the gullet. The shark's swallow reflex engaged, and the muscle plate she sat on angled downward. In she slid, her last vision of the July day above the spectacle of Jim's head sailing high into the air, up to its apex before dropping down into the pool shark's mouth. She turned away, and let herself slide into the abyss, and found it cool, and spacious, and only slightly stinky.

DOLPHIN PEARLS

The dolphins played beneath the soaring arches of the intracoastal bridge. They twined around one another, just a thin shell's edge away from touch, and then lay on the surface for a breath, beak to beak, and felt the sun dry them. The stickiness of salt skin, tacky, where jawbone meets another sinus. They fell back from one another and accelerated into the diving game, tail fin high up in the air.

et

On the day Miranda's mother went away, in the local swimming pool, Miranda hardly wept. She was stunned, a 14-year-old lanky and shivery in the tiled corridor. Her mother, Cassandra, chose a spectacular way out. At the end of Cassandra's aqua fitness class, elbows still vibrating from a vigorous sequential jog, Miranda's mother jumped up, up, higher, and higher. All around her, her elder friends looked at Cassandra, the relatively younger woman in their midst, their mascot fairy, their light one, smiling and twirling to the Elvis beat. Cassandra smiled back, beatifically. People told Miranda later that Cassandra spent a lot of time with the swimming pool mural, porpoises in mid-jump over the waves, the realistic rendering surrounded by the starfish imprints of countless 3rd graders' small hands. Cassandra had looked at the mural hard, focused, as if there was something to decode among the reds and greens, the yellows and blues of these fingerprints, the plastic whorls holding on to the DNA of a whole community.

Then, that day, during the aqua fitness class, Cassandra started to sing, her throat opening wide, flaring beneath her pink lips, tongue twisting upward, engorged with the luscious purple blood of ancient vibration.

Miranda heard her mother's singing, heard the eerie sound while fastening her shoes in the corridor that ran along the back of the pool. She put her feet down hard, and her teeth clamped shut, too. Then she raced round to the wet passageway that led to the pool. She screech-turned around a wall of green tile. There was Cassandra, her mum, surrounded by a gaggle of aqua fitness elders. Her mum's face was turned up to more fully extend a throat like a cormorant's red sack, billowing like the sail of a sunship that glides between the stars.

Miranda jumped in the water, paddled to her mother. She knew it was urgent. She needed to get there. And she made it. The moment she arrived at her mother's warbling form, the sound nearly exploding her ears and chest, Miranda dived under and made for Cassandra's feet. There they were, light green in the cool light of the pool bottom. Miranda could see the webs beginning to form between the toes. Then Miranda extended her own small white hand, like a twig in the water, and used her short nails to clip the near invisible rope that held her mother's ankles to the pool bottom. The leash parted, translucent ribbons sinking to the pool floor, the remnants shaping bracelets around Cassandra's sturdy ankles. That was all that was needed. Miranda burst up through the blue water, pushing out a placenta's worth of water from lungs and trachea. Next to her, her mother's singing subsided slightly. The folds of neck gills retracted into yellow skin. And then she shot up, amid a geyser of pool water, loosened and open, a shrill note in the air. Cassandra was gone.

None of the pool elders knew what had happened. One or two stared at Miranda, as if searching her for fire, for rockets, for blasting caps. Only one elder, a blue-haired lush half swaying in the water, looked at the community mural, and traced with her hand the back fin of the nearest dolphin.

Miranda had burst into tears and was inconsolable, first in the pool, in the drafty corridor where she waited for her father, and then at home, in the quiet, dark, empty rooms where her father first cried, then drank, then told her stories of mermaids and sea mammals, and the terrible price of land legs.

er

Today, on the pleasure cruise boat, was the eighth anniversary of Cassandra's rapture in the pool. Miranda, motherless orphan, watched the dolphins, her hands twisted and white around the tourist boat's railing. She felt her balance shift with the curvy roils of the mammals just off to starboard. For a second she relaxed her own grip and felt the salt stick on the tender palm of her hand. Then she resettled, grasped, keeping herself from mounting the rail and jumping high up to the sun, deep down into the green wave.

Miranda congratulated herself on her level-headed denial of those desires. Just like passing up a cooling gin and tonic, the tinkle of ice cubes like giggles in her ear. Like passing up a genteel glass in the local gallery's exhibition opening, Chardonnay slipping in past murmurings of pastel appreciation. She was strong, and her feet were firmly planted on the astroturf of the pontoon deck.

Behind her, Miranda could hear the Argentinian couple bickering about stars, and inlets, and, maybe, far away islands. Her Spanish was rustic, and not up to these round rolling sounds. With eyes and heart she sent love vibrations to the white-haired woman, the one who quietly looked at the passing scenery, only interjecting here and there a comment into the waterfall of her speaking spouse. The dolphins continued their play off the boat's side, and now they had come up close, quite extraordinary close, and there they were, heads rearing up from the waters. One's beak was just so to the side, like an intelligent poodle judging her owner. Miranda stared at the dolphin's eye. It held her. It commanded her. It pushed her forward.

Later, one of the bystanders on the boat would report how the young woman who had so desperately clung to the railing suddenly let go, opened her handbag and started the ritual.

Miranda took out the rosary. The dolphin looked on, curious. Still standing upright in the water, its beak opened from time to time, as if preaching. Miranda tore the rosary's silk string. Individual wooden pearls gathered in her palm. The small silver crucifix at the end of the string cut sharp lines into her tender flesh.

The dolphin wanted it. Miranda took the crucifix, and dug deep into her face.

The other dolphin caught on to the game aboard and began running antics behind its mate. Standing high on its tail, it roared backward through the waves. Miranda did not pay attention. She was right then about eight years old, firmly attached to her father's hand. They had visited a Disney park that housed a sad-eyed giant dolphin, an Orca. Miranda and her father visited the underground aquarium wall, and she held her small hand against the cool thick pane. The orca swum nearby, its black and white skin shimmering in Miranda's vision, obscured by tears. Meanwhile, her father told her about rape in the dolphin world, about gangs of juvenile males ravaging one of their sisters, about blood in the water, about how nothing is as innocent as it looks. When they went up to the surface, to the dolphin show with its finale, the orca jumping out of the water and splashing the audience, Miranda wasn't able to see the mammal through her tears. At home, her mother, the poet, scolded her for being morose, for being withdrawn, for being a loner, and how her father was fed up with the both of them, the sobbing women, the treacle stickiness of family life. Miranda wrote down these words in her diary that night: Treacle. Morose. Gang rape.

On the boat deck, Miranda succeeded in opening shallow cuts on her cheeks, little pepper stings of tribal scarring. The fellow boat passengers shifted backward in horror as the first drops of blood fell thick and dark onto the green turf. Miranda was still looking at the dolphin, only taking her eye away to select the first two beads. Then she inserted them carefully under her dermis. The dolphin chattered at her, sensitive jaw vibrating in the drying air. Miranda felt the air's coolness on the new braille beneath her skin.

Miranda finished inserting the prayer beads. She felt sure that her future love would understand the message, etched in blood and pearls. Her fellow cruise passengers shrunk back even more as the young woman grasped the rail, swung a foot on the lowest rung, and then stepped like a gymnast up to the top bar. One man, a recent transplant from Colorado looking to make his home in the surf shops of the barrier island, reported that the young woman had reminded him of Rio de Janeiro's Sugarloaf Jesus. She shone, he kept repeating to the coast guard men. Another passenger, recently returned from her first trip to Havana, remarked on the music floating in the air, a cushion of sound that seemed to surround the boat like a light fog, a swaying deep in the hips of the keel.

After that moment of suspension on the rail, Miranda dove down into the waters.

et

None of the fellow passengers could quite agree on what had happened, and the interviewing Coast Guard officers sat over a beer that night, redacting their reports for the official record. Had the dolphins really approached the young woman, lifted her hair with their beaks? Had they twirled around her, offering fins to her groping hands? And had they truly towed her away from the boat, out toward the far islands beyond the horizon? They didn't believe a word of it, and knew that a long day of search lay ahead of them, poles and bright lights lancing into the coves where the manatees rest in the warm waters.

Privately, the officers dreaded that amid the searchers would be the one remaining member of this stricken family, Hector, Miranda's dad, Cassandra's husband, dark eyed, army fatigues hitched over belly, the strength of a luchador still tingling beneath dark tattoos.

The coast guard veterans remembered the weird story of how they had found Hector in the swamp. Oh yes, that was, to the day, exactly four years before his daughter's jump off the boat, four years after Cassandra disappeared from the pool. Hector was found huddled, mud-smeared, in the root cave of a mangrove. They remembered the wounded bellows of the once powerful man, now under constant suspicion after the vanishing of his wife. They recalled the barks and whistles of an exhausted larynx. In his belt had been a knife and a diving bag full of abalone. Tucked amid the plump shell flesh, provenance unclear and hence occasion for instant rumor, was a rosary. A tiny crucifix haloed with pink pearls nested in the moist flesh-folds, ancient sand corns that had grown more and more luminous with each passing moon tide.

The Coast Guard officers extracted Hector from the root labyrinth, and he had been silent, drifting. They brought him to his home, where his teenage daughter sat beneath the kitchen table, clasping the wooden leg, a tableaux of pity and grief.

Not knowing what else to do, they left them there, father and daughter, with the father's hunting bag. For the next week, till the stink became too much, the bag of mollusk flesh oozed fluids onto the kitchen table, sticky and drippy. From what the officers could figure out when they visited later to check on their charges, father and daughter just spent their days looking upon the miraculous rosary and the pearls, marveling at the drying liquids transforming colors into flesh.

er

The dolphins played in the dying light. Their beaks broke the surface of the still water, their dorsal fins lancing through golden evening streams. Their numbers fluctuated with the seasons, predation, the patterns of migration. Whale lovers joined, and floated away, new babies were born. Today, a creature of green-blue whiteness glided among them, and breached in the weeds.

THE WAVE

The rogue wave scaled the sky. The sea moved beneath her. She pushed upwards, her arms churning trowels in the glossy water, her legs sucked down by the gigantic mouth of the undertow. If this skyscraper were to break over her, she would be pushed right through to the calm cavern beneath the ocean. Mara cut off the scream building behind her teeth, sour tastes of copper adrenaline and sea salt coating her tongue. A quick look behind her showed her yacht, the Jolly Maid, still upright, calm in the trough between giant waves. She did not understand. But she needed to stay focused, conserve her energy. There was no way to get back. Paddle. Paddle up against the rising swell. Crest the monster. Mara pulled, each arm rising above the dark green waters like a defiant flag. The giant wave roared back. It took her.

&

Much earlier, Mara had stood on the deck of the Jolly Maid on her way out of St. George's haven. She was all alone on her route out of the harbor. Other boatmen gave the Jolly Maid a wide berth. Which puzzled Mara, but suited her just fine. All the groomed, silver-tipped, widow-peaked men could get lost, keep their money and their advances, and stay behind in the bars of St. George. She was in charge, alone on her new boat. The sky ahead was wide and blue.

Mara didn't look back, didn't see her boat marking the smooth surface of the sea. She didn't see the women on a distant dock, their heads strangely bowed, standing in half-mourning.

Mara loved the feel of her new jeans on her skin, her sheath against the knife of the world. No more sequined bikinis on this boat's bridge, little plastic edges digging into the tender spots above the swell of her breasts, or into her upper arms, pressed close to her torso. Cool smooth blue cotton soothed fading blotches of black bruises. Martin's handiwork, still with her months after she had walked out. It had taken so many visits to the Battered Women's Center to regain her own balance, to build up to leaving Martin, her love, her husband, and then to stay gone, in a new world of supermarket shopping and dinners for one. Now, she was prepared for her own sea legs. She was going for the wide ocean.

Mara remembered the day it had started. The day her transformation began. Nothing had been different. Martin had been gentle at first, funny, full of jokes about weather and the laws of the sea while he steered his powerful yacht. Blond hair in the wind, curls flying. He told her a story about a people under the sea, mermen diving beneath stone arches, freed from the dry air of their coastal towns, and of a giant godhead waiting to wake deep beneath the waves. Martin was such a raconteur, had her shiver and giggle at the same time. Martin's storytelling talent had thrilled clients at company dinners in Providence, over lobsters wormed out of their shells and guzzled with hot fat. Listening to his silky voice, she loved him and his life. She loved the yacht, the dinners, even the flesh of lobster spiders, the acrid tang of martinis on her tongue. He had let her into this life for a small price. Their bargain was spelled out, before their wedding night, as near as it could be without words. Mara was to be an exec wife. Do not embarrass me. That's all I ask of you. Do not make me look bad. There will be lobster and pearls, but do not embarrass me in front of anybody.

She had gladly acquiesced. Never did she want to disgrace her elegant Martin. She loved her long fake fingernails, the clinging silk of thin summer gowns, the velvets of winter, the dew of her own skin, smooth and gorgeous.

But then Martin had changed their bargain. She could see the pressure in the new white wrinkles around his eyes. Things were hard, the economy drifting like seaweed, fewer dinners, fewer clients. The lobster spiders got smaller, and, like the fishermen fishing beyond their quota, no one wanted to talk about it. The hustle came in, new pressures. Agendas had shifted, for him, and he had new roles for her in his life.

After the story of the godhead under the sea, a casual wave had tipped their yacht just a little. Mara had tipped off balance, laughing, and her drink had spilled all over herself, but also, oh no, on him, on his firm belly, his six-pack of early morning gym muscle. Her drink dripped onto his canvas shorts.

He had lashed out, in one fluid motion, quite casually, brushed her aside into the sharp pipes and hard edges of the leeward stern. She had cramped in pain, writhing on the deck. Her head slid out beneath the rails. The sea. Down below had been a green calmness looking back at her. She had hung there, suspended. For a moment, she had wished for this calmness, mermaids cruising in languid spirals.

Martin wasn't done, though. Once started, he followed through. Beating her was to be his sport, this morning, on a slow yachting day with nothing much going on, no clients to entertain. The skin on her cheek finally split as Martin's hand drove her into a metal edge. A single blood tear rolled warm over the bridge of Mara's nose, hung for a moment on her nosetip, and dropped down into the green water. Mara had looked down for a minute longer and said her sea prayers. Then she pulled herself together, back onto the deck.

Just before she got up, a sudden wave had leaped up from the warm waters beneath. It had drenched her silk dress as she sat on the mahogany planks. Patches of bloody skin had burned with the infusion of the salty sea, burned bright and hard. Some of these patches were on her face now, for the first time. The burn brought it all home. Mara knew that it was decision time. Her assets were in danger, her beauty all she had to pay for the life she wanted. Her currency was tanking.

She had rolled over, looked down once more into the green, seeing the sun dance in spider webs on the merry waves. She thought of sea gods. She thought of scars on her face, and the breach of their contract. She did not like it, but it had to happen. As small white crowns skimmed the waters below, she decided to stand up.

When she turned away from the sea a dark fountain of water had bubbled upwards. It wetted the place where she had lain. The column of water swallowed the few drops of blood that had fallen from her small wounds. Then, slowly, the watery tongue had dripped back down from the deck to its mother ocean. But Mara had already been hobbling below deck to scream at Martin to bring her back to land. Martin had been stunned by the change in his wife's demeanor. He was tired. He needed a drink. Thinking about it, he didn't like what his hands did to her beautiful face. Something was broken, in him, in them, and he knew it. He laid his trembling hands on the steering wheel, and carved the ocean back to harbor.

et

The visits to the Battered Women's Center were demeaning and frightening at first. Most women were local. She was the only stranger who had felt the pull to join a group of fellow survivors—never victims, the group leader reminded her—of domestic violence. The rickety club offered a respite, small old tables full of home-cooked food, a few mismatched chairs, dark curtains against clean windows. Few slept here, most just visited, having snuck out of their houses, in this town where so many men let out the frustrations of a diving economy on their women's hides. Mara encountered women who were oh so different from her, who wouldn't know the order of plates and silverware at the golf club. At first, she had been disgusted by the smells, the sights, the unraveling her nose and eye seemed to perceive in the colorfully dressed women who had joined the circle.

Then there was Talira, lithe and wrapped in red and yellow cloth, a slight hobble telling of her drunken fisherman husband and his fists. Talira had been the first one to talk to her, one beauty to another. Mara had been awkward, hesitant, even frightened to tell too many tales from home, lest it might interfere with her divorce proceedings. She didn't quite understand the lawyer's talk, confidentiality, what goes where. Talira had stopped her attempt at small talk, after a while, eyeing her tongue tied conversation partner. Then, she had held out her wrist to her. A thin white line shone against the dark skin, crossing over old traces of abrasions, zigzags of knife lines, even small circular burns. Mara had looked, and had lifted her own brown wrist, without a small white line across the wrist. But she knew what the line meant, and yes, it had happened to her, and yes, sister, I see you. Yes yes. Tears leaked out of her eyes, and Talira had brushed her cheeks.

Over weeks of visits, Mara had rallied, had abandoned herself to the surge of energy that lifted her spirit every time applause rolled like thunder in the round after a woman had found the courage to speak out to the group. But, like many, Mara didn't speak. She had sat amongst them, thin hands clasped in front of her. The others had left her in peace, left her to find her own time to speak out, and to pour her voice into the ocean of women's strength. But she just couldn't make herself do it. Her voice was stuck deep inside her, stuck on jagged edges of pride and guilt, in a well of sadness.

After the sessions, Mara had come to see the social events as opportunities to reevaluate her reactions to the women: she had become used to the smells of baby powder and household cleaner, to the dust of factory floors and the hints of cheap perfume. As they ate cookies and homemade cakes around the rickety tables, she had come to see a different gracefulness, reared so close to the sea. She noted the fluid motions of hands touching, of a lock being tucked behind a brown ear, a white ear, voices rising like bubbles from deep wells. After these meetings, Mara would go back to her hotel room, her new home after leaving Martin's side. Sometimes, she dreamt of Talira. Mostly, she dreamt of a dark green sea, dances in underwater ruins, then a maw, teeth like stalactites draped in seaweed, slowly closing, closing, and the feeling of ivory daggers in her back.

The other women at the Battered Women's Center, having waited for the new one to depart, gathered up the remaining food and wine and walked slowly down to the old docks in the run down parts of the harbor. As they walked, their fingers twined dried seaweed into wreaths, ready to send out onto the waves. The familiar actions were smoothed by time, half-automatic. Some taught receptive newcomers their craft. Mara was not receptive, not yet, might never be. They whispered to the initiates about their small sacrifices. Some of the women, one of them Talira, looked back, secretly, up the street to the tourist quarters, but none crossed the line and talked about forbidden things. It was too early to invite her. Mara would have to listen to the call first and come of her own accord.

And in her bottomless sleep, after these draining afternoons, Mara heard ocean sounds which she couldn't remember in the morning, and she woke full of pains in her midriff.

et

The Jolly Maid was offered for a great price, tucked away in the small ads one dreary Tuesday afternoon not long after Mara's divorce came through. Mara had answered the newspaper advertisement, strangely eager to own a boat, any boat. This desire was new to her, but so exciting. She would be in charge, would transact what needed doing, would surprise her divorce lawyer with her oomph. She hadn't been on the sea again after that last day with Martin, but at night she longed for the green light of the deep, for the calmness, the gloss, of liquid solace, for the salty kiss.

The smooth male voice at the other end of the telephone line had agreed to meet her at the minor marina where the craft was anchored. The seller, Skipper Hein, was a tall, lanky, quiet fellow whose hair or eye color Mara wouldn't have been able to describe afterwards. Somewhat blond, somewhat blue, but with a shifting pearly sheen, a peacock's glitter in the still air. He gave her the shivers, for no reason she could see. He was friendly and his hands did not linger too long on her flesh. But she did note the slight webs between his fingers: an unusual anomaly, but harmless. His voice was a pleasant hum over the waves.

They had been alone on the gray, grainy wood of the walkway. It seemed unlikely to her that no one else had shown any interest, but maybe this minor location down from the main piers had deterred other incomers from looking at the small yacht. The business was quickly transacted, cash changed hands, most of Mara's divorce settlement. Mara had registered her new possession and bought books to learn about boat handling.

As she cleaned her new water home, she noticed strange patterns that had seeped deep into the blond wood. The paneling around the cabin bunk was stained with streaks and splashes. Small pools of darkness eddied beneath the fixed carpets that Mara took up, exerting herself with considerable trouble, pouring buckets of sea water on the old wood. She scrubbed the wood by hand, with small brushes, and in the seams she found where grime of different colors alternated once enough flushing water had loosened old patina. Nearly invisible, long faded, the darker colors fascinated Mara, who started to invent histories for her new craft as she cleaned and scraped.

A deep-sea fisherman wrestling with a giant ink-spouting squid. A retired sea captain smoking away his life in the tiny cabin, and spitting past bronze spittoons brought all the way from India. A family of four, headed by one of the women from the women's center, cramped into the boat, their only and un-likely possession, clearing fish-guts and slimy scales in order to win their daily bread.

For the first two weeks of her new ownership, Mara's head spun tales out of the manifold meetings of men, women and the sea, the tales growing ever more vivid with every night spent in the comforting confines of the bunk, the boat securely an-chored in the marina. As she lay there in the darkness, once her eyes had fallen shut, the stains below her bunk, deep in the wood-grain of the yacht, subtly changed shape.

Finally, she took the Jolly Maid out of the harbor. White foam leaped past her boat's silvery side, like porpoises guiding her out into a new realm. Mara told her new friends at the wom-en's center that she was ready to leave.

And her friends had smiled, nodded, and looked at the silk-clad lithe woman in their midst. They told themselves there was nothing they could do, and they shushed Talira when she tried to speak up. Mara had become one of them through pure chance, in the split-second of a deadly joke played by the mighty sea, accepting an involuntary blood sacrifice. They knew the sea was now ready to settle the score. She was Hein's, they whispered.

Talira, in particular, knew and ached with the knowledge that this woman was lost to her. Mara's hands, so different from her own, roughened by rope and nets. Mara's dark eyes, looking into her own light-colored eyes. Why couldn't Mara see the dan-ger of Hein and his yacht? Hadn't she paid attention, seen the seaweed wreathes, felt the need for sacrifice? The town's history had stilled Talira's tongue, or else she would have warned the incomer, told her about Skipper Hein, about what to do with this draw to the sea.

Mara couldn't see it. But in the lines of women's deep wrinkles, sea prayers lay hidden, full of worry. They had quickly recognized the source of change in Mara, her new strength, her resolve and ability to leave Martin's battery. In their hearts, they recited the old chants that keep the spheres apart, the elements, the different realms of humans and the powerful sea. Mara hadn't seen the warnings, hadn't learned the chants they sang in the full moon at the water's edge, didn't know how to weave a wreath, how to load it, or where to launch it to keep the merpeople appeased and in their watery space—hadn't learned the rules of her new strength.

Ranj, one of the older women, tried briefly to speak out and warn, seeing Talira's distress. But Mara couldn't listen to her low voice, the downcast eyes, as Ranj tried to speak of the sea-floor mysteries. All Mara saw was another old sea woman, or maybe a shy domestic, one of the workers, trawler-women. She, who so recently had been awed by the sea town women's fluid grace, now felt pity for them as her heart swelled with a call to come out, to come out and play, to be alone on the green waves.

Finally, Mara gave some dollars to the mumbling Ranj, lifted her hand in a good-bye, stuffed another handful of dollars into the collection tin on the desk, and strode out of the center.

Mara felt Talira's gaze on her back, felt it like warm fingers stroking her spine. For a split second, she hesitated, felt an opening into a different future, shivered under the eyes' touch. Talira of the red drapes, the fringe over a brown belly, the wrist's thin line, jasmine smells, light liquid, eyelash wonder, soft.

But this story had happened too fast, and Mara hadn't taken the time to listen to any alternatives. The Jolly Maid was calling, its freedom, contract-less, open and inviting like the waves. Mara's momentum forbade her to turn. Sad eyes followed her, soft moans, and fingers were weaving seaweed.

er

The provisions were stowed away below deck. She had enough fuel, all instruments and machines checked out at the harbor. Strong, sunburned men had looked askance at her as she ordered them around her boat. They didn't speak, but Mara sensed their discomfort, on being ordered by a woman, and by a woman her race—a discomfort she wanted to recognize as her due in a white man's world, now that she stepped out of the shadow-life of being a man's wife.

Her cropped hair rippled in the wind. The wind's movement on her loose fitting jeans created the same sounds playing cards make in young boys' bikes. The sea lay like a mirror, and her boat carved a white trail in the harbor. She never looked behind her at the hieroglyphs in the green sea, and only a lonely woman on the shore read them and cried into her red shawl.

For two days, paradise held. Mara slept soothed and becalmed by the waves of the sea. Beneath her the dark patches crawled and took new shapes. Small amounts of sea water seeped in through insignificant cracks, not even enough to fill a tea cup, but they wetted the darkness, merged with it and expanded, making their sign deep in the fabric of Mara's yacht.

The third day out at sea, Mara woke to a dark sky hanging low above the upset waters. A white flash of lighting on the horizon wedged itself between the sky and the sea. The storm was coming closer. She knew what to do in stormy seas, had even taken a certificate course. But now, when it counted, she couldn't do it. Her feet were glued to the boards, wouldn't shift. She reached down, her frantic hands pushing against the air as if caught in molasses. She tried to lift her foot from the deck. Nothing. Something like roots reached down, from her skin and bones right down into the deck. Mara tried to scream, but her torso constricted around her, pressed her lungs to her spine. Her eyes wide in shock, she stood on the deck, her stance seemingly relaxed, with a gentle sway like an old seadog, hips and knees in unison with the sea below. Far back in her brain, Mara well recognized the danger she was in, thoughts scrambling like rats on a sinking ship. She recognized that she needed to act, do something, or at least radio in if she felt unable to avoid the storm. But then her brain turned, and the larger, older parts of her brainstem held a different message. Against her frantic pinging, long, old nerves rooted her to the spot, on the wooden deck amidst a thrashing sea, drinking in her intensity, her fear, her sweat.

With supreme effort, she willed her eyes to leave the line of the horizon, and she looked down to her feet. There, a congealed mixture of dark red liquid and sea water oozed out of the deck, forming a dirty puddle around her. She still couldn't lift her feet free of the disgusting mess. The waves of the sea were crashing right across the deck of the Jolly Maid, but they did not seem to touch this fetid mixture, did nothing to wash away the stain on the blond wood. Neither sigh nor scream pushed its way past Mara's constricted throat. Her skin puckered and tingled with the smell of blood and salt all around her.

She stood, rocked, nearly fell. Hours. The storm drenched her. Her clothes ripped into shreds. She felt the fabric's touch on her limbs, wet eels snaking around her legs. Mara stood, and suffered, and held against the storm. Colors played across her memory: green and blue, and red and yellow, dark as bruises and tender as palms. The colors leached out of her eyes and into the hungry waves.

ꝏ

Skipper Hein stood on the marina looking out at the storm. He laughed, high and piercing. Women in their homes heard his laughter. They pulled the bedclothes tightly over their heads, blessed the strength in their arms even as they cursed the source of their energy and resolve. Their toes curled away from the sea that danced only yards from their brittle cabins. Their nostrils were full of the sweet salt stink.

Skipper Hein knew that the Jolly Maid would be found again, all alone out at sea. He knew what the townspeople were going to say: it had been a bad luck boat ever since the first blood had been spilled on it, a woman from far off Houston killing her husband and her father-in-law one sunny day out on the high seas. Previous owners had been washed overboard in stormy seas, as was likely to have happened yet again, or had killed themselves in accidents or suicides on board. Some voices would yet again call for the boat to be burned. But, as had happened on previous occasions, Skipper Hein knew that he would buy it back from the coast guard, who were going to be happy to have it taken off their hands.

And the day that Skipper Hein motored the yacht back to his bay, women would stand on the docks, their feet planted on the gray wood, arms stretched out and hands full with wreaths, fruits, cake and flowers, dripping colors down into the calm waters. Their eyes would be glazed, some even hostile, but their heads would turn slowly, unwilling, to mark Hein's passage. And he would chuckle, glad to have them quiet, to pray and scatter their useless trinkets. Whatever they did, another one would break free again, would answer the lure, and feed the deep kingdom with her dreams.

et

Finally, the end approached. Mara's feet became unstuck as a giant wave licked across the deck. Cartwheeling, she crashed into the sea. Her back bruised with the impact, remembering the dream teeth far below the sea. Her mouth opened, and salty water ran deep into her lungs. But the paralysis of the deck had passed, and her limbs obeyed her as she tried to keep her head above water. Breathe, air and water.

The Jolly Maid, miraculously still upright, danced on the waves behind her. But the sea pushed her away from her yacht, out into the gray darkness. She turned away. There was the wave and its tug. Her blood called deep below where the green fades into black.

The Libation Ceremony

She got bitten. Again. Dana slapped, frantic, trying to hit the insects that angled at her from all sides. Every inch of her rosy flesh tingled in anticipation, histamines roiling her blood. Sun, sweat, and the bite of eucalyptus insect spray wafted close. She was ready to pack up, get her gear out of here, find a hotel to get away from the insect-infested swamp.

Sapelo Island lay ahead, mosquitoes whirring around her head as she looked out, still uncertain about whether or not to stay in this bower. She imagined the old plantation slaves: faces, wrists bloated from mosquito bites. Her host had told her how farm workers here in Georgia's lowlands need to clad themselves from head to toe in tight-fitting jersey, dense enough to hinder a proboscis's probing. But though she kept looking out for strangely garbed insect people, she only saw people, white and black, dressed like herself: dusty jeans, workers' boots, loose t-shirts.

But she had seen a line of five raccoons, swimming across the salt marsh. Likely, they had been trapped on a marsh island, rudely interrupted in play and feeding by the encroaching tide. No one else was swimming, no human footsteps showed up in the beach muck.

Did people ever swim here, immersed in brine to head off itchy bites? To wash off the sweat and muck of the field? She looked out of the dock gazebo. Her foot knocked her cane loose from its lean against the rocking chair. Nothing but reed water all along to the next island, a darker line against the horizon. Farm homes glinted in the sun. People enmeshed in agriculture, as long as the salt water didn't rise too high and poison the farm.

Suddenly, the gazebo rattled, water splashed. Dana looked over the railing. Nothing. Again. A splash, followed by a red-orange butterfly ascending from beneath the dock. Was something underneath her? A touch of unease filtered through her curiosity. She tested the railing carefully, then scanned the waters.

It floated into view for a second, then receded beneath the bleached wood of the dock. It trundled out again. Dark, light, shadow and watersun sparkling on an ancient face. Dana could see it clearly now. It was no corpse. There was no smell. No ancient ghost. It crept forward again, nibbling the grasses, feeding. It was a turtle, a huge old monster. In its shell was a face, a skull embedded in horn. How could a skull fuse with living horn, accreted and grown on a terrapin's back? Dana stood transfixed by the white of bone in the darkness of the horn. Patterns and scales had grown over and into the white hollows. The skull's jaw was missing, and only an uneven row of tooth-shaped shine remained, level with the upper margin of the turtle's back. Above that, the triangular hollow of a nose, the flaring of sinuses, a bulge of forehead integrating into the downward swell of the turtle's back end. Dana wondered if this was a species. If so, how could this adaptation provide an advantage to the feeding turtle? She hobbled to the chair, grasped her working bag, took out charcoal and paper, and began to sketch.

The openness of water. Dana tried to capture the marsh scent, the fertile roil of matter down liquid paths. Each day, she sat here at the turn of the tide, not far from her artist residency home on this Georgian barrier island. Today minnows cascaded past the deck, swept in by the salt rush of the ocean. They divided, shifted direction, collided head-on with another branch. She tracked the fish delta, tiny bodies glued to the shifting edge of the rising water, nibbling nutrient sediment. Over time, the swarm rolled downstream, each curvy shift in direction inexorably leading down, always down. She pictured the front-most minnow, wedging itself in the tide river's head-waters. Would the mud taste different, there?

Sheet upon sheet filled, grey and black, her fingers smudged and agile. And beneath her palm, the curve of the skull's cheek-bone drifted up to her from the rag paper.

She collided, saw herself give up control of the steering wheel, the concrete bridge, the motorway divider, the bridge's railing. She saw the blooming airbag, the helpless smears, felt her scream stuck in her opening throat. There was never another car, as she recoiled from involving someone else in her fiery imagination.

A dark dragon, out in the marshes. Dana rustled her sketch-book. It turned toward her, to the flammable dryness of the dock. A red eye, a giant snout opening, a flame tongue, breath, rushing toward her, unimaginable pain, her skull, collapsing, black tissues, splinters, sheets of charcoal adrift.

Reds and liquids. She felt the texture of burgundy over rough asphalt, fingertips in drying flecks of matter. Capillaries of soil received her warmth. Her blood, mingled in the tidal flat, painted delicate coils downriver to sift through foreign gills. A shark, far out at sea, the last recipient of her hormones. Fish-tongue memories of older blood, bodies thrown overboard, dark skin oozing around iron manacles. Dana drew, connecting the shapes of organs and the effluvia of labyrinthine shells. She drew, and her heart calmed.

That night, Dana lay caught on the other side of sleep. She took her cane and walked down to the deck on the marshes, the stars inked milk above her. At night the deck sounded different. Fish jumped. The waning moon slid over the high tide water, its ripples distinct and rushing. Sleepily, she sat down in the rocking chair, her toes searching for splinters and nicks in the old wood. The deck held the day's sun against her feet. A smell, fetid, sweet. A crane croak, far off. Dana rocked. Nodded.

A breeze came up. Rushed past her. On the breeze, laughter. Two girls. One in white, a pale ghost on the deck's railing. A tug of war. Snatched curls. The other's skin took in all light and gave none back. Dana could see little snatches of cotton fabric, washed pale. A nightdress, patched, with an uneven, ripped hem.

Dana sat in the rocking chair, and watched the moon-shadow girls play, drop their clothes, jump into the night river, climb back out on the dock steps, swing themselves from the railing, jump, jump, splash, jump. Water pearls and droplets of laughter, all quiet, all silver, all skin. Dana looked on, tried to see the patterns of lace and tatters, to grasp the night-sweat deep in the threads. Saw the stretch of the girls' young limbs, spines arched over the dark water, reach, fingers splayed, the release, the coolness of the marshy seawater. Mud caress. The sharpness of reed as they climbed back out, hands grasping each other's to help themselves back on the deck. Danger electric under their feet: discovery would likely mean a scolding to one of them, but to the other, crippling pain, torture, the lash. Furtive quick looks, no disturbance, no stirring from slave cabins and the master's house. If the two girls talked to each other at all, Dana couldn't hear it.

Toward morning, Dana stretched. She had fallen asleep, the patterns of the old wood of the backrest now baked into her cheek. She massaged her face. Checked herself for ticks, bites. Some welts. The sun was emerging lilac and red over the reeds.

She limped to the railing, leaned out. In the lavender light of morning, she searched for the old turtle, but it did not come out. With the warm gold bruising the far horizon, Dana retraced her steps back to her ranch, shuffling through the Spanish moss. She felt the morning mosquitos bloom around her, blood penance.

A few hours later, still before the heat of noon, Dana stood on the beach at St. Simon's Island. She lead a phalanx of four women, three nut-brown with aged suntan, one powdery chocolate. All five of them stood tall in their bathing suits, bare feet curled into the sandy bottom of the ocean. The outliers of warm, brown Atlantic waves washed gently over their insteps. Dana called the tempo to their walking, inviting them to breathe through the bottom of their feet, to reach down toward the earth's core.

"Claw your toes into the sand butter. Enjoy the sensation."

The group stepped forward, one foot at a time, found ground as they anchored their hips over their knees. The ocean pulled on them, back, forth, their spines releasing and adjusting in unison.

Dana stood with her back to the incoming waves, monitoring her students, her cane abandoned on the beach. All four had their own response to the tidal pull. Karena's legs were splayed outward, lowering her center of gravity toward the earth. Her eyes were closed, and she was blissful, her pink suit encasing a full form, soft white rolls undulating in the muscular heaves of the water.

Angelica was tighter in her hips, her knees closer together, eyes fluttering open to check her posture. Dana smiled at Angelica, took note of her stiff grey-blond hair, the tight belly beneath the green lycra. Dana breathed into her own belly, releasing, relaxing, and saw a slight give in the older woman's midriff. Good.

Next to her was Cora, a merry widow from Hong Kong, in her sixties. Cora's feet lifted up from the sea floor, met each wave with their own foot twirl, happy to ignore instructions that did not follow her particular path toward oneness with the ocean and the earth. Her energy and enjoyment travelled outward, her less than perfect form undoing any sense of 'doing it right.'

Pulled along in Cora's flow was Cecilia, the youngest, and the newbie in the group. She was still shy, figuring out if this form, the improvisation of grace under watery assault, was a good fit for her. Her stripped suit spoke of the leaness of lane swimming. Her close cornrows glistened in the sunshine, and her form was excellent.

Dana stepped up the tempo, doubled on the wave's action, enjoyed her knees' response, the absence of pain. All followed suit, hunkering down to stay secure. Breath rates increased, and Dana knew they were in the zone. Some beachgoers stopped and looked out at the group, thigh-deep in the waves. Any further out, and the ocean would have been too pushy. Dana stepped the group down, back to a rhythm aligned with the waves. The next part of the class was ocean walking, moving through knee-deep water, focused on balance and spinal flow, letting sensations run through and over. Her favorite part of class. All five turned, stepped a bit more toward shore to drop the level of their immersion, and began their walk. The poise of their necks spoke of peace, even in Angelica, who stepped without hesitation through the surf like an emerald crane. To their side, ocean-bound, pelicans roared in, ready to dive.

They were now lined up with the first town café, their point of turn. Dana moved to the new front of the line, her arms swinging, pushing the tempo up to aerobic. She felt stable enough to step backward for a distance, smiling encouragement at each of them in turn. Legs in double beat, arms open to draw in the salty humid air. The tide was coming in. The shoreward push of the water increased sideways pressure on her calves and thighs. She fell back a bit, to be level with her first two students. Karena laughed open-mouthed, delight in her eyes. Cecilia smiled, too. Angelica and Cora pulled alongside, straining against the matrix of water. Karena whooped, and Cora joined in, a band of explorers. They grasped each other's hands. Then, they all stopped, without signal.

A line of five women, hands linked, breaths rising and falling. Dana could feel Cora's heaving next to her, her porcelain hand shifting up and down with the exertion of breath. The ocean battered them from the right, but their bodies were flexible, reeds and willows. Her knee whispered of pain, but withheld, in balance. Energy hummed. Dana listened with her back, with her feet. Mollusks rolled in earth tunnels deep beneath her toes. The lines stayed and swayed, stabilized.

Cora saw it first. A slight pull on their arm-line, an intake of breath. It came in from the open sea, each wave drifting it closer to them. It ran across the crest of the wave, licked by water at the apex, then trundling down. There was movement in the arm and leg holes, but it was blurry, indistinct. It was the turtle Dana had seen yesterday at the deck, the skull shell. For a moment, the turtle crested upright. The white skull grinned out at the line of women. The eyes looked out, the upper jawbone that marked the bottom edge gliding into the water as if the skull took a deep draft. Now Dana saw the turtle itself. The red eye-line of the living turtle head whisked back and forth, tasting the airwater. The next wave. The skull shell shifted into horizontal, losing definition. Drifted.

The five women stood in the water now, the rhythm forgotten. Cora and Karena were clasping hands, bosoms heaving. Angelica was still, white cheekbone planes under bronzed skin. Dana was reluctant to look at Cecilia's face, to read what might be legible there on Cecilia's black skin, what look might shoot out to her from dark eyes, and she was ashamed.

Slowly, Dana started up again, pushing her legs like pistons into the murky water. The other four followed, spread out, walking in the knee-deep sea. After a while, they marched out, stretched on the drying beach. They took their leave. Dana retrieved her cane, purse, and wrap. No one mentioned the skull shell. Dana's mouth was dry, separate. They moved to the beach's exit. On the glistening sand sat a horseshoe crab, armored legs trembling, on the edge of death. Dana thought of dinosaurs, an order of cruelty before humans. She wished she could send the creature on its way again, lift the heavy shell, carry it tenderly back to the waves. But she wouldn't do it. It might bite. It might stink. It repelled her, these rounded segments of alien life.

In the car park. They dispersed. Angelica in her sparkling Ford. Cecilia got a lift back to work with Cora. Dana saw the ease of connection between these two, the laughter. She raised her hand as they passed. The mosquitoes were on her again, and she opened her own Honda's door.

"Dana. Wait."

It was Karena. A Hawaiian dress of big Hibiscus flowers covered her wet bathing suit, with a ring of moisture sparkling her neckline. She held her water bottle in her hand, pink plastic with a screw top. Karena's voice broke through the egg-shell thing that filmed Dana's skin, quietly, a soothing wave sound of thanks for the classes, her delight in moving in the salt water, lyrical descriptions of float and the joy she felt, here, in the noonday fall sun.

Dana listened, still, a light lean on her cane, mesmerized by Karena's sensations, the shared feeling of salt on skin, the shift of water against blood. A tear tracked down her cheek.

Eventually, Karena stopped. She raised her water bottle, unscrewed the top. There was nothing to say. Dana stiffened, took a full breath. Karena looked to the sea. Both women listened to the wave's beat vibrating the shore. Karena poured her libation to the dead. The trickle of water wet the car park's sand. Both closed their eyes. The turtle skull drifted between them, bodies in water, labor on the land. The blood beat of the sea, the mosquitoes' whine.

Time passed. They opened their eyes, and the sounds of the beach car park started up again. A seagull screamed overhead.

Dana felt her knees, her hips, asking for rest. She barely caught Karena's quiet murmur.

"Please, repeat."

Karena spoke louder, carefully pulling her white English tongue around unaccustomed black speech.

"Ebeebodee got a right ta de tree ob life. Hunnuh mus tek cyare de root fa heal de tree."

She shrugged, apologizing for her awkward pronunciation.

"That's Queen Quet," she added.

Dana recognized the name of a Gullah-Geechee leader, a willow woman who led ritual in Savannah's Juneteenth celebrations, visited with local colleges, presented her people to the United Nations. She repeated the words, with Karena's help, thinking of the willow woman's presence, the cadence of her speech, her song.

"Hunnuh mus tek cyare de root fa heal de tree."

They did not know if these were the right words to honor the dead, the gulf between. But on the thirsty ground, the sweet water found its way into the earth.

The Viking Ship

It rose out of the mist. The slender bow spiraled into a circle. Its sharp edge parted the moist air. The carved wood on the prow's leading edge scythed through the water. With a crunch, the vessel ran aground in front of me. I fell back, landed heavily on the sand. What was Viking ship doing here, on a deserted tropical island? I had seen ships like these before, mounted securely in museum buildings near Oslo, whitewashed walls to hold the dark timbers of ships that had been buried as mausoleums.

There had been one of those dead Viking warriors displayed right next to his wooden shroud. The forensic anthropologists had had a fantastic time with his skeleton. The small white note attached to the wall informed me of two different swords hacking at his legs, cutting him down in the middle of a fight in the approved Viking way of maiming one's adversary. There had been no remodeling of bone: this fight had been his last.

So far, though, I couldn't see any longhaired warriors jumping off the big black boat that had just materialized in the foam off this beach. Just the sinuous shape and the sound of the wood biting into the new land. I couldn't see any oars, either, just the round holes where they were supposed to be. I noticed something else weird, too: there was no sail. The mast in the middle of the ship had been ripped off, or snapped, and was just a few yards high, not enough to blow any ship across the ocean. This was an empty shell of a Viking ship, more like the excavated and cleaned-up exhibits, not something pulverized in the screaming furies of the Atlantic scour.

I repositioned my wooden leg. The beach was hell for me. Little grains of sand kept coming in, find their way between the protective sock and my skin. If I wasn't very careful there'd be blisters and aggravation and no leg to stand on. So I carefully shifted myself through this undulating sand world. I could do with some good company, even company that howls and displays a lack of table manners—anything better than the daily emptiness of this god-forsaken island.

The ship had come up on the beach far enough for me to take a peek without risk of losing my leg underwater. So I moved up, touched the old wood. Its tar felt sticky in this tropical heat, and it smelled like oil. A feral stench. I imagined a crew living among these fumes.

There was not really any way to get up this smooth overhang of wood. I needed a different plan. Back in the cave was a long rope, something I had salvaged from the Jolly Maid, and also some finer yarns and plastic ropes I found stored away in the empty aircraft that had crashed over the mountain a while back.

I turned back, left the black ship on the beach, and limped up the gentle rise of a sand dune to my cave, a shallow declivity in the cliff. I fashioned a sort of anchor: a heavy rock, attached to a rope. The rock had to be able to counterweight me, and yet needed to be light enough for me to lift and lop over the railing. I was getting there. So I returned to the boat, still silent and menacing on the wet sand. I moved as far down its flank as I dared, to where the wide flare of its deck was most accessible. There, I twisted the stone up, and threw with all my might. I was so glad that I didn't have to do that more than once. The rock obediently took up position on the deck, and, upon tugging, lodged itself firmly. Ready!

It's hard to get up on a boat with a wooden leg. You can't really clasp a rope well, or mold your thighs to the contours of the wood and shift upward. At least that's how I imagine you are thinking of getting up on the deck, winning a few feet, before hooking a leg or arm over the overhanging deck and shifting, grunting, muscling one's way in.

I don't really know how it all works. I lost my leg too recently to have a good road map of how to work with prostheses and stumps. The leg got cut off by a hungry shark during a storm. I am still not sure how I managed to not only claw my way out of the waters but also stem the blood streaming off my stump with a belt, in the water, in a storm. But I did it. All alone.

On my little rescue island, I knew I had to come up with some solutions to my new limb configuration. So, once I managed to light a fire with my small smoking-days left-over lighter in a buttoned shirt pocket, I sterilized a needle from the first-aid pack that had drifted to shore. I closed arteries and veins, knitting them shut like rubber hoses. Yes, that was painful. They threatened to slip back into my flesh. I had to hunt for them in my stump, veins like salmon hiding under rocks. Anyway, we did it, vein fish and artery salmon, sewing needle and the remnants of blue yarn from an old sewing kit, in the poor firelight of my first flame on the island.

I have christened the island Sigrunn since I wanted a clean name, an easy one, no kings or explorers. Sigrunn felt so European and princess-like, so light and Vespa-touring, so right for my little spot of heaven.

Then it was about a month later. I was not very good at tracking time. I did the cut notches into the wall thing for a while, but then I got a fever, and wasn't well, and it was a hassle, and who cares. Eventually I was fine, the weather was good, there was water, I made a wooden leg, and I ate too much fish and fruit. That was a lot better than being shark food. But it was also boring, hence there was me trying to get onboard the Viking ship.

My fingers and arms were really strong by now, all that gripping and fishing. I hauled myself upward, hand over hand. I touched the rim. I grasped it, firmly, the wood solid and clean underneath my arm. Scooted higher, threw more and more of my stunted body toward the edge, and then shifted over the edge, head first, torso, squishing boobs, then the remaining leg bits spilled into the vessel's interior.

I came to rest with my arm hook twisted, my whole body draped over more oil-covered tarlike stinky wood. There was no one up there, on the deck. The deck was clean, empty, devoid of life and its little traces. No dinner stuff, debris, old plates or wooden mugs rolled around. The sea had claimed everything. Some seaweed draped across the old steering oar. This was the only oar that was still in place, all other holes were empty. But this huge beast of an open ship had made its way to the island.

I limped over to the mast, saw the splinters still raw from where a storm, or maybe some giant beast, had bitten it off. Everything, even the open wood wound, was covered in black tar. It pooled on the deck and slithered down the mast remnant. Next to the mast, the tar was thick, and it stuck to my home-made sandal, sucking at my wooden extension. I placed my leg a bit further away, to a thinner coating of the thick slime. This was not pine tar, the stuff Vikings used to waterproof their rides. This was something else, less wholesome. But it had done its job: there was the ship, in one piece, riding high.

So I stood there, a bit off kilter so I wouldn't get myself stuck. I thought firewood, if I had a way to dismantle the ship. There was nothing of value to me to collect, no hammer or nails or in-struments, never mind stored food. It all looked clean and shiny black under the tar, all in one big wooden piece. Before disap-pointment could track up my leg and into my bowels, sinking my heart again, I heard a sound from the stern. Or what felt like the stern, given that the dragon boat was double-headed, with two ornate coils on each end. The other side. The side away from the beach. The side still hanging over the ocean drop off. The side I hadn't been able to visit since I arrived.

I went forward. Climbed awkwardly over the rowing seats. Avoided accumulations of the black slime. I was at the back end. I shuffled my weight backward and forward a bit, bit paranoid, making sure the dragon boat was firmly wedged into the sand. I did not wish to suddenly go on another journey, with all my hard-won possessions left behind in the cave. It seemed solid. I leaned over the edge.

Below: giant tendrils, kraken arms, fire hoses, water snakes. I quickly retracted my head, back into the boat. Not fast enough. Something had spied me, something that clung onto the Viking ship. It darted over the edge, up and over, downward, and pinned me. I screamed. High pitched shrieks pierced my ears: that's me, that's me howling, after all these weeks of little tears, that was now me on full blast, terror, horror, fear.

But the release did not end the nightmare. Something had pinned me and I couldn't quite figure out what it was. This grey-pink arm thing was thin at the tip, this tip that explored my exposed skin. Then it got bigger, thicker, but it still looked like a worm, no suckers like an octopus or squid. The tip searched, probed a bit rough. And rougher. And then I could see it

I can see it oh no it is doing it open up my belly something splits and it tastes and goes in and there is red and white and yellow fat and coils glistening

I heard my own scream thin and really high. After much too long, it retracted. It moved backward, out of me, creeping bit by bit out of the grey yellow red mess I could barely look at. And as it retreated it shuffled over the skin, like there was some invisible knitting going on, and right enough, my belly began to close. A sci-fi show operation. Star Trek laser-beam cut and dice and close. The grey-pink tendril was out now, fully out, and inched back toward the black slime-covered balustrade, as if retracted by something satisfied and done down there. My belly ached, but only in a crampy kind of way, like my period was coming on, the kind of pain that is half nerves. I tried to stand. No harm done. But I could see spots of blood glistening in the sun on the black wooden deck. And even a fleck of yellow matter, belly fat, flicked out like a discarded morsel. I walked to the railing and looked over. There was the creepy mass, tendrils, worms in a giant coil. I could not see how they connected but I am sure they did. There was something about the whirling movement that told me that they did, that they were sucking one brain thought juice. I was certain some brain or nervous system had steered the dragon boat and had come for me.

Eventually I got back to my cave. It was really hard: I was disoriented. My leg really hurt. Some sand grains had made their way into my improvised stocking and prosthesis, and my skin was raw and bled a bit when I finally lay down. My belly hurt, too. I was out of it for a bit, I think.

The ship stayed around, and I could see it from my cave, like some giant black ferry stuck to the rim of the blue-green lagoon. It called me. Every day, I visited, but I didn't go to the far side at all. I got strong from shimmying up the rope, tested my leg, gained balance, even grace. I explored the whole ship, looking for clues of its people, or where it came from. I admired its lines. The graceful arc of its bows. The economy of its planks.

Today, I am ready to take it out. My supplies are in the boat now, the small amount of non-fish food, any container that can take the dwindling water from the dying stream behind my cave. I thought about a chart and tried to spy on the stars high above me. But I kept falling asleep, not knowing what to look for.

I can see the sun now reflected in the black tar of the ship. I tried to scrape off some of it, to clean at least a small area for me to sit and steer. But no luck. The ooze shifted right over and under any knife I took to it. No amount of water would loosen the smallest speck. So I sit on the black stuff now, feel its warmth heavy and liquid against my thigh. My wooden stump leg got stuck in it many times as I was exploring and provisioning, so I am now leaving it off. My scar rests right on the covered wood, and I think it takes comfort from the warm hint of smoothness.

I created a glorious contraption to get the ship off the sand, an arrangement of boulders and wooden spars that will allow me to heave and shift the heavy stern once the tide is just right. For days now, I've been waiting for that high tide.

The water rises around me. I am off the ship, my shoulder hard into the largest piece of lumber that connects the rock pivot to the black knife-edge of the dragon boat. I push. The water soars. I am soaked, my bare white leg stump stretches away from me, tendons taut, my belly tight with muscles and fear, my breasts draped over the stone. I do not want to stay. Do not leave me. I am leaving. I am leaving. Finally, movement.

I climb up the rope I had left hanging over the railing, shift upward and over as the black boat roars backward through the crashing waves. We crest the waves, shift back, back. I put all my new strength into the rudder oar, turning, turning, back muscles straining. At last, we face into the wind and the surf. Without sail, without oars, we are underway. The black sap runs liquid, eats all the light. Its warmth is like the sweetness of a home fire.

Night falls. I see the island fall behind me, green seam on the steel sea, and then it falls into the horizon. A drink, a handful of food. I fall asleep at the rudder.

A rosy hue of morning breaks over my eyelids, and there is movement in the corner of my eyes, around my bare stump, a flicker and lick that is gone when I look closely. Hints of movement. More water, food. I think about fishing, adding to my supplies, but the dragon boat is steaming under the ocean's own steam as if in full sail, as if staffed with twenty-four strong men pulling and pushing on oaken spars. Too fast to let out a line. I stand at the prow and look toward the horizon, a curve out into the warrior land.

After a few days the water runs out. My fruit have long gone. I am hungry, but the flesh of my stump burns with life, burrowed into a mount of black tar. The mount supports me as I stand, eyes out, face into the wind. We draw nearer to the edge. The visits last longer now, and I can see the worm taste finger lick on my flesh when I awake, seconds of whirling mass stroking my flesh and the wood and the tar.

Now I feel it inside. An anemone, unfolding tendrils. A longing. Worms blossom in my heart. Vibrations, fibrillations, like a high-pitched song from beyond. I stand and sing along, my bones humming, pearly and pink inside my shrinking flesh. My stump pulses within the tar, warm and connected. Worms wriggle everywhere. My limbs are alive. I am upright. Blackness flows into the small channels of my skin. It covers my hair. We stand, eyes open to the sea. We stand and sail toward Valhalla. The worm is ready to stand up in the fight. We are coming.

FIELD NOTES

Whenever we try to envision a world without war, without violence, without prisons, without capitalism, we are engaging in speculative fiction. All organizing is science fiction. Organizers and activists dedicate their lives to creating and envisioning another world, or many other worlds—so what better venue for organizers to explore their work than science fiction stories?
    —Walidah Imarisha, foreword to *Octavia's Brood* (3)

This is a book of disability culture reclamation. It reinvents myths of otherness, and it reaches toward the party place, toward interdependent webs between humans and non-humans. This does not mean that all the stories are about disability, or feature it—instead, I am applying the methods of transformation I learned in disability culture worlds to claim old ground.

Activists and artists use tactics to reveal new opportunities for living. I learned from reading Afrofuturist stories and from sitting in story circles, from feminist techniques and queer kinship retellings. I am queer/cripping old stories: I don't reject them, or break them. Instead, I use tools of transformation to reshape how we can think of agency, how bodyminds can align with shifting myths, environments, and pressures. I nudge old sites of horror into surrealist shapes. What does it mean to crip Nordic myth (Viking Ship), pirate yarns (Vicki's Cup), urban/rural dystopias (Playa Song and Ice Bar)? How can I work with Lovecraftian Mythos material, without just disavowing their misogynistic and racist impulses (Dinosaur Dreams and The Wave)?

A number of stories in this collection come from working in/with/about asylums. I am a wheelchair-using disability culture activist, and I often work with mental health system survivors on site-specific performances in old asylum spaces (including Seacliff, Aotearoa New Zealand, once the largest institution in the Southern hemisphere). My partner, Stephanie Heit, a poet and dancer, lives with bipolar mental health difference, and has lots of experiences with hospitalizations, including memory loss from shock treatments. In 2015 to 2018, we ran the Asylum Project, workshops which invited community participants to share what the term 'asylum' meant to them, using writing, movement, and meditation as our modalities.

One day, we were at the old Traverse City State Hospital (also called the Northern Michigan Asylum), which is now being recast as a shopping space. I found a book in their cellar bookstore—this became the start of a story (Grave Weed). Other landscape descriptions in the stories here come from a Dutch asylum, Duin en Bosch, which we visited as part of our performance research, and Eloise, an old asylum near Detroit, Michigan. The stories honor lives lived in asylum space, deep history, old pain, and the ongoing tragedy of institutionalization. How can spheres thought of as separate mix and merge, what uncanny effects happen at new surfaces?

Other core themes woven through these stories are women, water, and power. Much of this collection was written while the Dakota Access Pipeline protests were at their height, and I read daily of police and state atrocities, of precarious lives, as well as about the power of ritual and community in movement organizing by native people, by Black Lives Matter activists, or #SayHerName organizers. During these writings, I witnessed local Anishinaabe Women Water Protectors in their ongoing work to honor water and life. In Ice Bar, I explore connections between women and water in multiple ways, while trying not to appropriate stories outside of my own cultural circle.

What are the grounds for new utopias, what do journeys to the stars look like now, for someone like me, as more and more white people and settlers like myself scrutinize the foundations of our myths and entitlements? I crip the little mermaid while paying ecopoetic attention to the histories of the Bay Area (Road under the Bay) and use gender/science theorist Donna Haraway's thoughts on making kin to explore yet another mermaid (Dolphin Pearls). Other stories use water to narrate transitions (River Crossing, Playa Song), and drift in watery realms of memory and history (The Libation Ceremony).

These stories shimmer our narratives of borders into unknown, differently inhabited territories, using the tools of speculative fiction to open up to weird reading and writing practices.

Here is this collection's invitation to you. Take up your own storytelling ability: imagine the world differently. Take a story that obsesses you, and shift it so it reaches toward the contours of the world you want to see. What values power your story? Where do you place your emphasis - on narrative drive and a moment's deliciousness? What mysteries are central to your universe? Find others to read to, to write with, to imagine together. What can bodyminds do, in this new world? What do they do to socialize, to hang out, to take a load off, to celebrate being alive? In my world, I'll see you at the Ice Bar.

GRATITUDE

Thanks to the ancestors, the water keepers, the land guardians, my grandmothers, aunties and parents in Germany who told me stories while we visited forests and lakes.

Thanks to the worldwide Olimpias community and our local Ypsilanti, Michigan Turtle Disco folks, the frames and supports for creativity in my world.

Thanks to everybody who participated in our Asylum Project workshops.

Thanks to Harbin Hot Springs for all the dolphin dancing.

Thanks to Neil Marcus for co-creating the Salamander Project, disabled people going underwater together and with our allies, and to the many participants who swam with me in oceans, lakes, pools and rivers around the world.

Thanks to many water and earth writers, for inspiration and rigor, including Donna Haraway for the story of the Camille Stories; to Walidah Imarisha and adrienne maree brown, co-editors of *Octavia's Brood: Science Fiction Stories from Social Justice Movements*; to Djibril Al-Ayad and Kathryn Allan, co-editors of *Accessing the Future: A Disability-Themed Anthology of Speculative Fiction*, to NourbeSe Philip's' *Zong!*, Christina Sharpe's *In the Wake: On Blackness and Being*, The Kino-nda-niimi Collective's *The Winter We Danced*, Ruth Ozeki's *For the Time Being*, Nnedi Okorafo's *Lagoon*, and many cli-fi novels.

Thanks to the artist residencies and sanctuaries that opened up a space for my partner Stephanie and me during my 2016/7 sabbatical, to write and be, explore fjords and deltas, manatees and leopard rays, and to live consciously in a changing climate and a changing world.

I was so glad to visit with Naropa University's Summer Writing Program and Eldorado Springs, to be hosted by Vandaler Forening in Oslo, Norway and PLAYA artist residency in Oregon, to visit with Beguines houses in the Netherlands and Belgium, to spend time at The Thicket, an artist residency on a barrier island in Georgia, to be welcomed at the Hambidge Center in Georgia when Hurricane Matthew crossed our path, to learn Watsu on the Florida Keys, to engage in aqua fitness pool classes in Fort Pierce, Florida; to go to the pool with disability culture activists at the Jewish Community Center in Toronto in the aftermath of the US elections, to watch ice and water mix at the edge of Lake Michigan, to write by the cresting river in Boise, Idaho at the Surel's Place artist residency, to journey in a Continuum Movement workshop in Los Angeles after Esalen was cut off by catastrophic rains, and to do aqua fitness instructor training in Michigan.

Thanks to the University of Michigan, in particular the Institute for Research on Women & Gender, and the Sport, Health and Activity Research and Policy Center who awarded me the inaugural Joan Schafer Research Faculty Award in Sport, Fitness, and Disability (I call this my Sporty Spice grant), to research and write about women, water, and wellbeing.

Thanks for the support of a University of Michigan ADVANCE Summer Writing Grant.

Thanks to fellow workshoppers in Sequoia Nagamatsu's Psychopomp sessions, in Michaela Roessner's Science Fiction and Fantasy Writing class, and Nino Cipri's sessions at WisCon.

Thanks to all my editors, and their careful attention, and in particular to Tod Thilleman at Spuyten Duyvil. Thanks to Miranda Jean Walsh, my cover artist, and the beautiful work she has created.

Thanks to Kristen Roupenian, Elise Nagy, and Denise Leto, for proofing and advice.

Thanks to friends who offered hospitality on our travels: Summer Rodman, CJ Wilson, Aliyah Khan, Gwen Robertson, my sister Jutta Sprenger, Judy and Roger Heit, Amber DiPietra, Sharon Siskin, and Beth Currans, cherished writing companion.

Thanks to my collaborator and love Stephanie Heit, Northern lake amazon, fellow water baby, co-traveller in the elements.

Petra Kuppers is a disability culture activist, a community performance artist, and a Professor at the University of Michigan Ann Arbor. She also teaches on the Low-Residency MFA in Interdisciplinary Arts at Goddard College. She is the Artistic Director of an international disability performance collective, The Olimpias; and has led horror and dark fantasy writing circles in Wales and the US since the 1990s.

Petra uses somatic and speculative writing as well as performance practice to engage audiences toward more socially just and enjoyable futures. She has written academic books on disability arts and culture, medicine and performance, and community performance. Her poetry collections include *PearlStitch* (2016) and *Cripple Poetics* (2007). She lives with her partner, poet and dancer Stephanie Heit, in Ypsilanti, Michigan, where they co-create Turtle Disco, a community arts space.

CPSIA information can be obtained
at www.ICGtesting.com
Printed in the USA
FFHW02n0440010918
48211512-51947FF